MW01490275

# But One Life

## The Story of Nathan Hale

Samantha Wilcoxson

Cover reconstruction of Nathan Hale by Cheryl Daniel of Digital Yarbs based on New York City Hall statue by Frederick William MacMonnies. Cover art by Ars Rönnei Media.

# Other books by Samantha Wilcoxson

## American History and Historical Fiction
Women of the American Revolution
Luminous: The Story of a Radium Girl

## Plantagenet Embers Series
Plantagenet Princess, Tudor Queen: The Story of Elizabeth of York
Faithful Traitor: The Story of Margaret Pole
Queen of Martyrs: The Story of Mary I
The Last Lancastrian: A Story of Margaret Beaufort (novella)
Once of Queen: A Story of Elizabeth Woodville (novella)
Prince of York: A Story of Reginald Pole (novella)

## Middle Grade Fiction
Over the Deep: A Titanic Adventure

# But One Life

## The Story of Nathan Hale

Samantha Wilcoxson

Copyright © 2022 Samantha Wilcoxson

All Rights Reserved. This book may not be reproduced or distributed in any printed or electronic form without the prior express written permission of the author. Do not participate in or encourage piracy of copyrighted material in violation of the author's rights.

ISBN: 9798437851722

Printed in the United States of America

"How beautiful is death, when earn'd by virtue! Who would not be that youth? What pity is it, that we can die but once to serve our country."

- Cato by Joseph Addison

# Prologue
# Coventry, Connecticut – 6 June 1755

*For we are his workmanship, created in Christ Jesus unto good works, which God hath before ordained that we should walk in them.*
– Ephesians 2:10

The babe was born squalling. It was the first and last time his screeching would cause his parents to grin broadly. His head was covered with soft peach fuzz, and his weary mother gently brushed her lips across it. She sighed in contentment, her work had been well-done.

'Would you look at that!'

Elizabeth was surprised by her husband's outburst just as she had allowed herself to relax. What could be wrong? Her mother's heart clenched. But Richard was laughing, and she sighed in relief.

'He has a birthmark just like mine,' he said, pointing at the back of the babe's neck. Still laughing to himself, he continued, 'When I was a youngster, did the other boys ever tease me.'

He shook his head in the way an adult shakes off childhood hurts. 'They told me that a birthmark at the hairline meant I was cursed by witches to be hanged.'

He was no longer laughing, but he tried to smile at his wife to lighten the mood.

'What an awful thing to say,' Elizabeth cried, squeezing the tiny boy closer to her bosom. 'Children can be so cruel.'

'Aye, that they can,' Richard agreed quietly, reaching out to caress his infant son's head. His smile reappeared. 'But this one will have no such worries.' He kissed his wife's forehead. 'God has already blessed him with a loving mother. What else might his future hold?'

Elizabeth smiled back at her husband before returning her gaze to the helpless infant. A shiver coursed through her body, and she felt love for the babe overwhelm her and threaten to cause her heart to burst. Her arms tightened around him as she vowed to always keep him safe.

# Chapter 1
# Road to Yale – September 1769

*What is a friend? A single soul dwelling in two bodies.* - Aristotle

My horse raced across the meadow with such fluid grace that I wondered if her hooves ever touched the ground. The sun was still pink as it rose over my right shoulder, and dew sparkled like diamonds as it was sent spraying into the misty air in our wake. I grinned and glanced back at my brother.

Never did Enoch push his mount to fly as I did. He preferred the safety of a steady pace and the peaceful opportunity to bask in the sunrise and awakening wilderness as it was before we disturbed it. Had I not forged a path ahead of him, he would likely say something like, 'Nathan, is not the work of God a glorious sight this morning?' He would sound a bit wistful, almost like our sister, Eliza, when she pointed out that she would soon be of an age to enjoy Coventry frolics.

I allowed my horse to slow to a stop as I waited for my brother to catch us up. The mare tugged a bit, not requiring rest just yet, but she did not know of the long journey she faced. Yale was two days' travel from our pleasant village, and we could not gallop the entire way. My hand caressed her strong, sleek neck, and I murmured appreciatively in her ear. Upon arrival at university, I would mourn her return to father's farm, but collegiates had little need for mounts and fewer places to stable them.

I watched Enoch wander slowly across the same meadow I had covered in a flash, and the words of Cicero came to me. 'Life is nothing without friendship.' Our tutor, Dr Huntington, would, no doubt, be pleased that the philosophical thought had occurred to me, especially while considering my older brother as he carried on what appeared to be a full conversation with his horse. Just as automatically, my mind retrieved the Latin. *Sine amicitia vitam*. I could hear Huntington say, 'Well done, my boy,' and I smiled, pleased with myself in this imaginary interaction.

'Come along, Enoch,' I cried when he was close enough for my voice to reach him. 'Do not tarry! We shall miss our first lessons should we travel at your pace.'

Enoch admitted as much with a lopsided grin and prodded his mount into a trot. As he came up next to me, he retorted, 'Yet we also shall not arrive should we gallop until our poor horses go lame.'

I laughed and conceded, 'As always, you have the right of it, my wise elder brother.'

He shook his head at my teasing, and we carried on side by side at a slow trot as the sun rose to warm the chilled Connecticut landscape.

We traveled mostly in silence for several hours. Occasionally, Enoch would point out a particularly colorful grove of trees. He loved the autumn season when God's handiwork was so fully on display. I spoke when I thought of something I had read or a conversation with a friend. However, not much came to mind that I had not already discussed with Enoch.

We shared a room at home, just as we would in our college dormitory. I could remember few experiences that we did not hold in common. Supposedly, Enoch had enjoyed a few private moments before my birth, but I doubted that he had any recollection of those nineteen months. My memories were almost entirely of the two of us together.

My earliest reminiscence was of us trailing behind our

father through swaying fields of golden wheat. It would grow much taller in soil that wasn't so rocky and shallow, I remembered our father telling us. At the time I couldn't imagine it growing any higher. I would not have admitted it, but I was already afraid that I would be lost should I lose sight of father's broad, strong back.

My favorite part of the day had come once I grew tired, and father would swing me up onto his shoulders. Enoch would try to walk a bit longer, as if to remind me that he was older and stronger, but he would eventually capitulate to weariness and reach out to be taken up in our father's arms. I had thought father's strength and energy infinite, never wondering, at the time, if he wasn't just as fatigued as his sons. Only now did thoughts like that come springing into my mind. Had I been a selfish, difficult child? All I had known was that I enjoyed the view from what had seemed astonishingly high in the air and that I loved my father. I wondered if my father ever thought of those days and if I would someday carry my own son upon my shoulders through fields of gold.

Father had pointed out birds that flew overhead and small animals that scuttled across our path. Enoch and I had been dumbfounded then that he remembered all their names and which ones we should try to capture to take home for dinner. Now, however, we two brothers scanned our surroundings for likely prey, the lessons from our father learned so well that they had become second nature.

Enoch had a gift for sensing when the sun was precisely overhead, and he stopped his mount to rest at that moment. I reached into my saddlebags, thankful for the bread and cheese Eliza had packed for us. She had been insistent that neither servant nor our stepmother see to the task. Only our dear sister could ensure the nourishment of her college bound brothers. The softening of Enoch's countenance informed me that he too was thinking of Eliza, but we could not risk our newly flourishing masculine independence to speak of it.

Instead, we settled under a tree while the horses grazed. We thanked God before we ate, each adding in silence a blessing for our closest sister. Enoch was ever the one to pray at the appropriate times, speaking to the Lord on my behalf as well. He would be a preacher, he had already decided. Though I shared his faith, I had not yet decided upon my own path beyond Yale and the new experiences and lessons I would learn there.

'I am glad we go to Yale now, and that we go together,' Enoch surprised me by saying.

'Of course, we go together,' I mumbled through a mouthful of bread and sharp flavored cheese. My brow furrowed at not understanding my brother's meaning.

He cocked his head at me, and his fair hair slipped into his eyes. 'What I mean is that home isn't the same, so it is right that we leave and forge our own way.'

It took some restraint on my part to not be flippant. I knew to what he referred but did not much wish to speak of it. 'You do not like our stepmother?'

Enoch's lips upturned only slightly. 'I like her fine, and she is a blessing to father.' He took a bite and gazed around as he formed his thoughts. 'But our homestead is changed, and her daughters will be leaving their aunt to rejoin their mother soon. I wonder what place we will take when we visit.'

I had not considered this. 'Will we be the strangers in our own home?'

'We will be welcome.'

'But it will not be the same.'

'No,' Enoch said in a low voice. 'It can never be the same.'

I thought of our mother, who had gone to God two years

hence, and knew that Enoch reminisced as well. We spoke of her no more than we had sweet Eliza, but we had no need for the words to be said aloud when we brothers resided in each other's minds.

Shaking ourselves free of memories, we repacked our supplies and carried on toward New Haven, our new home.

As we approached the coastal city, my chest tightened. In my fourteen years, I had never seen such a city, but my desire to appear more courageous than I felt kept me from saying so, even to Enoch. I felt provincial and began to wonder if I was ready for Yale.

I glanced at Enoch. He was fifteen, but I hoped that less fear was present in my own features than what I discerned in his.

'Have courage, Enoch,' I said, keeping my tone bright. 'You are the light, and this is your city on a hill.' I grinned, as did he, though I wasn't sure I had retained the intent of the verse. We nodded at each other and prodded our mounts forward.

We had little trouble finding our dormitory, it being one of the largest structures in the town. Red brick soared up four floors high under a roof that would have looked more appropriate for a large barn. I had never seen the like, but this was to be my home for the next four years. Therefore, I decided I rather liked it.

I could not say the same for the condescending upperclassman who directed us to our room, but that was to be expected. Enoch and I were the first-years, sent here to give former first-years the chance to feel superior to someone. We entered the space that had been assigned to us and felt mutual satisfaction in having something that was solely ours.

Well, almost. We welcomed first one roommate and then another by the end of the day. I put on a grand performance giving the tour of our room, needlessly pointing out the bunks Enoch and I had left empty and discussing how many trips to the wood stack would be necessary to keep a fire going in the oversized fireplace once winter blew in off the ocean.

'Isaac Gridley,' our first roommate introduced himself as his trunk was deposited near the door. When he learned we were brothers, Isaac determined that our Christian names would not satisfactorily differentiate us. 'Primus and Secundus!' he baptized us, and the nicknames stuck.

I would normally have bridled at having a moniker that announced my subordination to anyone, but Enoch would never think to lord it over anyone and our classmates soon demonstrated that they would not treat me as second-rate. Therefore, I was content.

The young man making us a foursome was Elihu Marvin, who spoke in quick sentence fragments as if too much occupied his mind at once. We settled into our room, each with a proud feeling of being an independent man for the first time.

Enoch and I had made sure to arrive on campus before the commencement services for the class of 1769, of which our cousin, Nathan Strong, was a member. Our father had remonstrated us to pay special attention to the Latin oration that cousin Nathan was to give. We were proud to let our new friends know that this accomplished upperclassman was a close relation.

We beamed and sat up a bit straighter when he stepped up to the podium. He, like the rest of his graduating class, was wearing homespun rather than the usual trappings of wealth that would be on display for a Yale commencement. They had agreed as one to set aside these British products to show support for non-importation measures being organized throughout the colonies. It seemed to me that they could not wait to graduate to become men. They established their ability to make important decisions and political statements right here at commencement. All were wholly dressed in the manufacture of our own country.

After the ceremony, we waited eagerly to greet our cousin and congratulate him on both his graduation and the eloquence of his oration. He was eager to join us as well and shared welcome news.

'I will be staying on as a tutor,' Nathan announced to us.

Enoch and I offered our enthusiastic congratulations, pretending that we were happy only about our cousin's career prospects. His grin and merry eyes hinted that he understood we would be comforted to have a family member close at hand, but, of course, we could not admit to such a feeling.

'Will you live in Connecticut Hall?' Enoch asked, giving away a bit of his childish inner thoughts.

I looked up eagerly, wondering the same but not wishing to give voice to my desires.

Cousin Nathan winked, a fleeting gesture that I was uncertain had occurred when I thought of it later. 'I will, though not on your floor.' He paused before grinning broadly. 'I shall be near enough to my young cousins that you will have help when you need it but not so close that I appear to be a mother hen.'

I laughed at that, and Enoch looked at his boots with his cheeks tinted pink. A group of friends moved past like a wave, collecting our cousin in their wake, and we watched him go. I wondered if Enoch and I would truly seem so grown up in only four short years.

A few days later, our lessons began, and I had little time to consider much besides our assigned work. Reverend Huntington had prepared us well, but my brother and I still spent much of our time with our noses buried in books or writing so much that my hand cramped.

I was shaking out my sore fingers when Isaac laughed aloud.

'You torture yourself unnecessarily for your perfect penmanship,' he teased.

Not realizing that anyone had noticed my habit of taking care with each word, each letter, I felt heat rush to my face. Enoch only smiled slightly and glanced at my paper. Even light banter made him slightly uncomfortable and uncertain about when a line was crossed into sin.

Isaac had no such concerns. He swiped my work in progress from the desk with a flourish, as if to put my vanity on display though it was only us three in our room.

'Come now, Isaac,' I said with forced calmness. 'I have put much labor into that translation, and I still must finish before tomorrow.'

He held it out of my reach, and I refused to make a scene of trying to capture it.

'Isaac, that is unkind...' Enoch mumbled.

I appreciated that he wished to stand up for me, but my brother was not assertive. I offered him a half smile and returned my attention to Isaac. His mischievous grin made me wonder how he intended to dispose of my hours of painstaking writing.

'It is vanity, is it not, Primus, to take such pride in beautiful letters?' Isaac asked in an innocent voice as he held my paper high.

I rolled my eyes before settling them on my poor, disconcerted brother. A thought seemed to give him courage, because he stood so suddenly that my work was in his hand before Isaac had time to snatch it away.

'On the contrary,' Enoch stated calmly, handing the paper

back to me, 'it would be sinful not to make use of a talent given by God's divine hand.'

My grin was irreverent, but Enoch did not notice. Isaac mumbled slight repentance, and we once again each bowed our heads over our books.

Scarcely had we regained our focus when Benjamin Tallmadge strolled in. Cousin Nathan had recently introduced him as one he felt worthy of our friendship and likely to have a bright future. One who would be a good influence, I knew was the unspoken truth, but I liked Ben despite that. Cousin Nathan probably didn't realize that Ben was so well-prepared for Yale by his reverend father that he was bored and unchallenged by his studies. He was more likely to lead me into nefarious deeds than Isaac, who seemed more the type.

Ben glanced down at my paper, offering a correction, and I smiled in spite of myself. I hated to be proven wrong as much as the next man, but Ben's casual assistance was never given in arrogance. It just all came so easily to him.

He took a seat and waited for one of us to inquire regarding his presence.

'Have you no lessons to complete?' I asked.

Ben sighed. 'No, and I despise feeling idle. Let us do something.'

I was close enough to being finished, so I put away my quill and ink, leaving my paper to dry, and turned to him. He had a grin and something else that he was clearly waiting for me to notice.

'Where did you . . . how did you get that?'

He laughed at my incredulousness as he worked to open the bottle of wine. 'Have you cups? Or something that can pass as such?'

I looked around the room as if I didn't know every inch of

it by heart, and Isaac took note of Ben's offering.

'Why, I just realized that I am done with my work as well,' Isaac announced with a sly smirk and the slamming of a book that made me cringe. Much as I looked forward to some fun, part of me wished to ensure that he had not damaged the binding.

Only then did Enoch glance up from his labors, and his eyes went wide. Ben was saying, 'We shall just pass the bottle around then.'

But Enoch was shaking his head. 'We cannot!'

Isaac and Ben only laughed. I looked at my brother and shrugged. 'What is a bottle among us four?'

'Elihu shall soon return.'

'Then it will be an even smaller portion for each,' Ben countered.

Enoch pressed his lips together and made a show of returning to his books. I loved my brother and had great respect for him, but I turned my back on him then and accepted the bottle from Ben's hand.

Isaac was peering at Enoch, and I gave him a look that told him to leave matters as they were. Instead of teasing my good-hearted but too serious brother, Isaac turned his attention to Ben. Though we were of an age, we all recognized Ben's greater intellect.

'Will we go to war then, Ben?' Isaac asked before gulping from the bottle. He had attempted to infuse nonchalance into the inquiry, and he refused to make eye contact. The room grew quiet just the same.

Ben took the bottle and swigged from it before answering. 'It is too soon to tell. British troops have taken control of Boston, but what may rise from this current discontent?' He looked thoughtfully at the ceiling, his blond curls glowing in the firelight making him look like something out of a renaissance painting.

My mind wandered to the work of Rembrandt that Reverend Huntington had included in our studies, and I had no more wish than the others to suggest an answer to Ben's inquiry.

Seeing that we each held our tongues, Ben changed the subject. Tension flew from the room as we complained of harsh Yale taskmasters and claimed to have talked to pretty girls. The bottle was soon drained, but Ben was not yet ready to take his leave.

'We need to know what is happening. The papers will have first-hand accounts. I'm going to have my father send some broadsheets,' he said. This idea moved him toward the door as if he would write to the reverend this very night.

Isaac just laughed, making him sound much too young to have been imbibing. Enoch finally looked up in interest.

'You'll ask for stories about Boston?' I asked as my brain slowly tried to comprehend.

'Yes!' Ben exclaimed, looking for all the world as if he had not drunk a drop. 'We should not only be studying the ancients and philosophy. The days in which we live are but tomorrow's history.'

I nodded. It made sense, but I was tired and thinking only of my bed. Thankfully, Ben did not tarry longer. He practically flew from the room to his own just down the hall, and I burrowed beneath my covers.

# Chapter 2
# Yale – December 1769

*Swell the anthem, raise the song.*
*Praises to our God belong.*
*Saints and angels join to sing*
*Praises to the heavenly king.*
*Blessings from His liberal hand*
*Flow around this happy land.*
Hymn by Nathan Strong

I had given Ben's plans little thought until he dropped a stack of broadsheets on my desk with a heavy thud. Looking up, I found him beaming down at me.

'I have asked my father to send them regularly.'

'Extraordinary!' I thumbed through the stack, in awe of the quantity and no longer wondering how Ben had become so erudite.

He pulled over a chair, and we began our perusal.

After a few moments, Ben murmured, 'Impressment of sailors in Boston Harbor . . . . Non-importation agreements . . . . Nothing new. Nothing escalating.'

'Are you disappointed?'

He glanced up and shrugged. 'I cannot be disappointed in peace. Yet, does it not feel as though we balance at the peak of a precipice and must eventually fall to one side or the other?' I nodded, realizing it was true even if I hadn't thought of it quite that way. 'It is the tension I wish to be free from,' he continued. 'One way or another. I wish I knew what world for which we are preparing.'

I rubbed my eyes, the tiny newsprint causing my vision to blur. 'Just so, Ben,' I agreed. 'Troops have been in Boston for greater than a year. How long can it be endured?'

The door swung open again, this time admitting Enoch. He immediately spotted the broadsheets before us. 'What news?' he asked as he dropped his stack of books onto his desk.

'Not much new,' I said with a shrug.

'Then it is a Christmas blessing,' Enoch declared. 'Why is it that the two of you look glum?'

Ben restated his unease with the state of things, but Enoch appeared less troubled.

'Do not borrow from tomorrow's troubles as today has enough that requires tending,' my brother reprimanded us. 'These events and our future must be left in the worthy hands of our benevolent Creator.'

I found myself agreeing with him just as I had with Ben only moments before and mentally thrashed myself for my inability to think independently. Suddenly, I wished to be alone in order to try discern what I truly believed, but our door was opening once again.

'Merry Christmas, boys!'

Cousin Nathan came in sounding like Saint Nicholas and carrying stacks of parcels. He needed only a red robe and halo of holly. The three of us forgot our discussion of current events and jumped up to surround him.

We had all been refusing to say how difficult it was to be at school while we knew our families were home celebrating our Savior's birth, but here was Nathan with our holiday cheer. He surely remembered what it was like to be away from family that first year, feeling homesick and not willing to admit it.

'Orange cranberry scones!' I could hear the longing in my voice as I unwrapped the paper. Oh, to have a few bites of sweet, homecooked food.

Even Enoch joined in the excitement. 'Mincemeat pie!' he exclaimed with a boyish sparkle in his eye.

We were like small children as we discovered gingerbread, smoked ham, and strips of dried beef. With the greatest of self-control, we waited for Nathan to chuckle at us and give permission to dig in. Happy murmurs filled the room as we tried to be satisfied with small bites that would make the treats last longer.

'And I have brought this,' Nathan presented a jug, and we all stopped chewing.

'What is it?' Ben was not afraid to ask.

Pulling it away from us as though to tease, Nathan answered, 'It is cranberry hot toddy.' He paused while we exclaimed and cheered our good fortune. 'To be enjoyed only under my careful supervision.'

His grin belied his sternness as he filled a mug for each of us. Isaac and Elihu appeared as if they had smelled our hot toddy on the breeze, and mugs were provided for them as well.

'Cheers to Nathan!' we toasted, clinking our mugs together before sipping the sweet, warm tonic.

Perhaps I would not see my father or Eliza this winter, but when I gazed around at the young men surrounding me, I was thankful for this new family with which the Lord had graciously provided me.

# Chapter 3
## Yale – March 1770

*The madness of mobs or the insolence of soldiers, or both, when too near to each other, occasion some mischief.* - Benjamin Franklin

Ben announced his question as he entered the room. 'Did you hear?'

Not desiring to admit my ignorance but wishing Ben would simply impart his news, I turned an upraised eyebrow toward him.

'In Boston,' he insisted, but this clue meant nothing to me.

He rolled his eyes in exasperation before continuing. 'A massacre! The troops fired on citizens in the street! Children, no less!'

I tried not to allow my eyes to widen in horror. Suddenly, I wished my father was near. What could I say? 'Will this mean war?'

Ben shrugged, and I was suddenly struck by the smoothness of his face. Weren't we too young to go to war? He caught my gaze, and I had the feeling that he was reading my thoughts just as Enoch often could.

'It may be our duty to defend our country,' he murmured.

'Great Britain is our country . . .' Wasn't it? I let my words trail off in uncertainty.

'Connecticut is your country,' Ben asserted.

I reflected on that. It was true. I had never seen London or any other part of England, but I knew the hills and valleys of Connecticut well. 'Still,' I voiced my thoughts as they came, 'this was in Massachusetts.'

Ben nodded, conceding my point. 'But if they can do this

in Boston, what's to stop them from doing it in New London . . . or even right here in New Haven?' He had jumped to his feet as his ideas propelled him into action.

'Here?' I said more to myself than to my friend, but it was Ben who responded.

'Why not here? If they can control a city like Boston, they might try New York, or even Philadelphia!'

I had never visited any of those cities and couldn't well imagine what they were like. It made me feel provincial and inexperienced. I was saved from responding by Isaac and Elihu bounding into the room. They and Ben fed off each other's enthusiasm for the news, though none seemed to know much about what had actually happened. I stopped listening to them but couldn't keep my mind from wondering that if shots had been fired in Boston what might happen next.

My eyes strayed to the papers Ben had deposited on my desk upon entering the room. 'Here,' I interrupted their gossip, 'let us discover what has truly happened before we debate who has the right of things.' I grabbed handfuls of the tightly printed sheets and disbursed them between us.

Isaac took his reluctantly, but Ben accepted his as if we were launching a treasure hunt. His eyes quickly lit up. Elihu flopped onto his bed and waited for the rest of us to inform him of our findings

'Look here!' Ben exclaimed, holding up a sheet with a large image and little text. 'This engraving is by Paul Revere of Boston.'

'Well, there you have it then,' Isaac said, immediately discarding his papers. 'You can see for yourself what happened.'

Ben placed the sheet where we could all peer down at it at once. The picture showed a row of British regulars with muskets pointed toward a crowd of people in the street. The bayonets were threatening enough, but it was the cloud of smoke that was most ominous. Dead men were sprawled on the ground or being held by their companions. I couldn't help but notice a storefront that proclaimed the presence of Butcher's Hall. Indeed, I thought.

I glanced up at my friends, wondering at their thoughts. Isaac's face was red, his anger bubbling near the surface. Elihu had already transferred his attention to the papers Isaac had discarded, but Ben appeared more thoughtful, as he often was. I waited for him to speak. When he did, I was somewhat disappointed.

'Let's see what the other papers say,' he murmured as he returned to his pile.

Isaac spun toward Ben, his hands in the air, as if asking why on earth we would waste our time. However, I concurred that we should be as informed as possible, so I looked down at the broadsheet in front of me.

'This one says, "A quarrel arose between some of the soldiers of the twenty-ninth regiment and the ropemakers,"' I stated slowly as I continued to read.

'Here it calls it a massacre, just as Revere did,' Elihu countered. I had a feeling that he and Isaac's minds were made up.

'This one calls it the King Street Riot,' I interjected, though I wasn't sure I disagreed with Isaac.

'John Adams has taken up the soldiers' defense,' Ben said without looking up.

John Adams, I thought. Was he related to . . .

'A cousin to Samuel Adams,' Ben added, predicting our ignorance. 'Perhaps he simply believes they deserve a fair trial.' His eyes darted our way and returned to the paper. 'Or he thinks they are not guilty of murder.'

'How could they not be?' Isaac exploded. His anger seemed intensified by the fact that Ben and I did not share it. 'Did you see this engraving?' He held up the sheet that he knew very well we had each just examined while Elihu's head bobbed animatedly in support.

Ben gazed calmly upon the image. 'We have no way of knowing if that is an accurate representation.'

'What do you mean?' Isaac demanded, looking at it again as though the still figures might have shifted to tell a different story.

'That is how Revere chose to portray the event, but that doesn't look like a riot,' Ben retorted without joining Isaac in his anger, and Isaac deflated a bit. Elihu looked back and forth between them with a speed that almost made me laugh aloud.

'But if we cannot trust the broadsheets . . .' Isaac began.

'That is why we must read them all,' Ben insisted.

Isaac sighed and returned to his task, but I wondered how we would ever know for sure what was happening.

# Chapter 4
# Yale – November 1770

*Its objects are to furnish the students of Yale College with incitements to literary exertion aside from the regular course of academic study, to provide the means of improvement in Rhetoric and Oratory, to give frequent opportunities for the exercise of these arts, and, finally to remove the distinctions of classes and promote among all the member of College harmonious and friendly feelings.* – Linonia Society

'You must sponsor my membership,' I whispered to Enoch. My hands were on his arms, holding him in place and reminding him that I was his favorite brother. 'Come, Enoch. You know I desire it more than anything.'

He cocked an eyebrow at me without saying that if that were true he would not have been granted entry into the Linonia Society before I had. I frowned and attempted to appear repentant.

'I will not neglect my studies,' I insisted. Now that we were no longer first-years, I had allowed my study habits to slide just a tad, but I would redeem myself.

'And?' he prompted with a lopsided grin.

I sighed. 'I will not patronize the pub.'

Enoch shook his head and rolled his eyes. 'Of course, I will sponsor you. They've already asked me to bring you.' He shook free of my grip and moved toward the door.

'Truly?' I asked. 'Why didn't you tell me?'

He looked over his shoulder at me, looking quite devilish for a future preacher and said, 'What? And miss your begging?'

He laughed and closed the door behind him as the pillow I

aimed at him struck it. But I couldn't be angry. Enoch had made his fun of me, but I would be joining the Linonia!

Ben was always talking about the debates held at their meetings, and they sounded so much more interesting than what we were forced to discuss in the classroom. I was never quite certain if Ben was purposely provoking my jealousy, but Enoch gaining membership had been more than I could take. Thankfully, I could always count on my brother.

Only a week passed before he escorted me to the room of James Hillhouse, who was the host of that evening's Linonia meeting. James was a serious, dark-haired student with a long, sharp nose that made him appear older than his true years. He nodded his welcome as Enoch and I entered.

'Ah, you've brought Secundus!' I heard one of my classmates exclaim, and I wondered if it had been Ben. Too many bodies were squeezed into the room for me to pinpoint the source.

'My brother, Nathan,' Enoch introduced me unnecessarily for I was surrounded by mostly familiar faces, and I felt a few slaps on the back in welcome.

As soon as the meeting was brought to order, however, the atmosphere quieted and my friends' countenances were molded into solemnity. The feeling was reminiscent of being seated in a church pew next to my father when I was a young boy. The formal opening of business complete, I sat straighter as my brother stood to speak.

'I present for membership, Nathan Hale, class of 1773.'

I wondered if he would say more. What was required? Must he give a character witness?

'I second the motion.'

'All in favor?'

A round of 'ayes' echoed around the room, and Enoch

smiled at me. It was done.

I relaxed and almost laughed aloud at how nervous I had been. James was already moving on to the next item on the agenda.

'Our discussion question for this evening is presented by Ebenezer Williams,' he announced with a nod toward the young man mentioned. 'Why are men more inclined toward vice than virtue?'

James placed his notes on the desk in front of him and peered around the room to see who might offer an opinion. The question rolled around in my mind as I, too, waited for others to speak.

Ebenezer, as the one who had suggested the topic, began the discussion. 'Men are driven by selfish ambition. As selfishness and ambition are vices, the results of them will also be vices.'

Some heads nodded. Others remained still and thoughtful.

'But ambition is not always a vice,' I was surprised to hear Enoch insist from his place at my side. 'Paul states to the Romans that "It has always been my ambition to preach the gospel where Christ was not known." Could this ambition have been a vice?'

I tried to keep my face neutral, as impressed as I was with my brother's point. Ben took up the thread.

'And a virtue can become a vice if pride or vanity is at its root. Who of us is unacquainted with one who desires everyone to know of their generous works?'

More nodding and murmuring. I thought of Mrs Dunbar back in Coventry, who delivered meals to the needy only when the streets were busy and loudly proclaimed her own deeds supposedly to spur others on to good works.

James, our host, spoke next. 'Does man's sinful nature keep him from being motivated by virtue? What hope do we have?'

I considered this, looking around the room at what I felt

were virtuous, intelligent young men. What made them - made me - virtuous?

'Are we willing to sacrifice our own desires for the sake of another?' Ben asked. 'More than that, would we lay down our lives for another, as Christ has done for us? If we cannot answer in the affirmative, can we say we are virtuous or are we driven only by vice?'

James responded, 'You have answered a question with three more.' He and several others chuckled, and I sensed that this was a habit of Ben's. As his friend, that did not surprise me.

Others continued the discussion as I considered Ben's questions. Was I willing to lay down my life if necessary? Why would that ever be necessary? How else might I know I was virtuous?

When each had contributed some comment, James turned to me.

'What does our newest member think?'

I could not sound as philosophical as Ben or as theological as Enoch, so I chose to end the discussion on a lighter note. 'What thing most delights a man?' I looked around at my friends before continuing. 'Do we delight most in what we ought to be ashamed?' A few nodded, quite unashamed. 'Virtuous men will take the greatest delight in virtuous action,' I nodded to Ben. 'However, what delights most men is getting money.'

The laughter of penniless college students filled the room, and we moved on to the next topic of discussion.

# Chapter 5
# New Haven – March 1771

*Better to die ten thousand deaths, than to wound my honor.* – Cato
by Joseph Addison

Plates and forks clattered in the dormitory cafeteria, where I sat at a table with Enoch and Ben. My rations consisted of a piece of dry toast with scarcely more than a sliver of butter, a small slice of beef, and beets that must have been in the root cellar from the previous fall. The emptiness in my stomach did not make this paltry fare more appetizing, but I dug in just the same.

Enoch nibbled at his toast, and Ben chewed a long while on a chunk of the overcooked beef. Our eyes met, and I shrugged. Enoch raised his brows as if asking, 'Well, what can we do about it?'

Ben, of course, did feel we should do something about it. He swallowed hard, and then held up his cup of water as if presenting a toast.

'We should protest.'

'Protest?' Enoch asked, looking warily at his beets.

'Yes!' Ben exclaimed, warming to his subject and attracting the attention of a few friends at neighboring tables. 'Let us take our concerns to the headmaster.'

A few voices were raised in agreement, and I grinned at my outspoken friend.

'And let's go get some more palatable fare!' one shouted.

'Our protest begins now,' Ben agreed. He stood, leaving the untouched food and dishes on the table.

Enoch looked uncertain. It was not his nature to leave things for another to clean up. I could imagine he was thinking of the poor kitchen servants that would have to work harder for the sake of our protest.

'That is the point,' I whispered to him as I stood to follow Ben's lead. 'Come, Enoch.'

My brother reluctantly joined us, stacking his cup and utensils on his plate before he would leave them. Ben was already at the door with a line of hungry students behind him. Enoch and I waited for the last of these to file out before we closed the door on the mess of a dining hall and marched into New Haven.

'Do not tarry, men!' Ben called from the front of the crowd. 'We shall dine at the Rising Sun tonight!'

I laughed, and Enoch managed to crack a smile as we rushed to catch Ben up.

The tavern keeper took in the sight of a dozen college men filling his dining room without comment. Some of us laid coins on the table to indicate our ability to pay, and he began doling out ale, which we gladly drank.

Several of our friends were wondering aloud why we didn't simply avoid the dining hall every evening, but Enoch gave me a look that I knew meant we would need to be writing father for more spending money. We would not be able to repeat this protest any time soon. Taking up the mug in front of me, I was determined not to concern myself with tomorrow's troubles.

My comrades seemed to share my thoughts. There were some present who I had never witnessed partaking of ale or spending a penny, but Ben had loosened our inhibitions and made us feel that we were doing something honorable. He laughed as he leaned back in a chair to observe the results. Catching my eye, he winked like the devil he was.

I chuckled and raised my glass to him. He waved to the proprietor and indicated another round.

Enoch whispered to me, 'We should go, Nathan, before things go too far.'

Shrugging him off, I shook my head. 'It is one evening, Enoch. We study and behave every other.'

He frowned, but I knew he would not leave without me. He lifted his second tankard of ale with a sigh, but he drank deeply.

Bowls of thick beef stew were placed before us with warm loaves of bread and plenty of butter. My mouth watered just looking at it.

'More butter on this plate than we see in a month in the dining hall,' someone said, and murmurs of agreement went around the table.

Conversation quieted as we all indulged in the rich food with little more than groans of appreciation and the clatter of spoons upon bowls heard for a few moments.

'They starve you Yale boys?' the tavern keeper asked as he slid another round of ale onto the table.

We hadn't even noticed his approach, so intent were we upon our food. We laughed uproariously at ourselves and took up the mugs.

I lost track of how many times they were refilled before we stumbled out into the street. Most of the students had left earlier, feeling the effects of the ale or afraid they would oversleep in the morning.

Ben, Enoch, and I held each other up and considered the path that led to our dormitory. Ben pulled us in the opposite direction.

We were singing, and I realized that I didn't know how that had begun. Even Enoch, his eyes a bit glassy, joined in with his smooth tenor. He already had the pleasant tone that was required for the incantations he would be responsible for when he became a preacher. As we stumbled down the street, I doubted this was what God had in mind.

We eventually made our roundabout way back to the dining hall. Ben detangled himself from we Hale brothers, almost sending us sprawling, and threw his hands up in the air.

'Has our protest gone far enough?' he shouted as though we weren't within arm's reach.

Enoch and I exchanged curious shrugs.

Ben gestured toward the darkened structure. 'Has our message made a difference? Will we be served better fare on the morrow?'

Enoch laughed at the ridiculousness of this idea and leaned heavily upon me. Ben was picking up something from the ground, and I shook my head to clear it.

'We should return to our rooms, Ben,' I began, but Ben was not done with his protestations.

'Here, my fine fellows,' Ben said as he placed a rock in each of our hands. 'This message they cannot fail to receive.'

He flung a rock at the dining hall windows before we could ask what he had in mind. I felt suddenly sober, but Enoch giggled and tossed a rock of his own.

I could not have been more shocked had Jesus chosen that moment to reappear on earth. I fixed my astonished gaze upon my disciplined older brother, but this only served to make him laugh harder. Ben's arms were around him before he could fall to the ground.

'Come then, Secundus! Are you one of us?' Ben demanded as if he were commanding troops.

I shook my head at Enoch, who was still struggling to

control his laughter, shrugged at Ben, and launched a rock at the dining hall windows.

When I woke the next morn, the sun was too bright before I even opened my eyes. I heard Enoch groan and knew that he too was attempting to rise. Isaac and Elihu chuckled as they strolled from the room, leaving us to fend for ourselves.

I tried to remember my morning schedule and wondered what time it was. Even if I was willing to suffer my own consequences, I couldn't leave Enoch to the humiliation of missed lessons and rumors of poor behavior. I struggled into a sitting position and peered toward my brother to gauge his condition.

Curled up like an infant, Enoch hid his face from me. Therefore, I was forced to stand. This had the benefit of putting the pitcher of water within reach, and I gulped thirstily at the lukewarm contents. It was intended for our morning ablutions, but I was in much greater need of hydration. After guzzling what I judged to be approximately half, I took the water pitcher to my brother.

'Leave me be, you devil,' he said by way of thanks.

'It will help you feel better,' I encouraged him, forcing the container into his hands.

He barely lifted his head, but he did drink. Water trickled down his chin and soaked his sheets, but Enoch didn't seem to notice. When the pitcher was empty, he handed it back and collapsed in exhaustion.

I was just considering what course to follow when the door opened. Rolling my eyes, I turned, expecting Isaac, but it was our cousin, Nathan Strong.

His presence sobered and embarrassed me, and I stood straighter, shielding my brother.

'It wasn't his fault,' I blurted before I realized that our good cousin was grinning rather than preparing to discipline.

'Rest assured, I had no doubt of that,' he said as he stepped to the side of the bed. 'Here, Enoch. This will help, and you will remember to guard yourself from bad influences next time.'

He handed both of us a piece of ginger root.

'Ginger settles the stomach,' Nathan explained. He had also brought a jug of water and plate of hard, dry biscuits. 'Come, sit up, Enoch,' he urged. 'You won't want to miss your classes. Consider that the next time you go out to the pub.'

Enoch groaned but allowed Nathan to pull him into a sitting position and place biscuits into his hand.

'Why do men enjoy drinking so much?' he whined, and Nathan laughed. 'I'm quite serious,' Enoch insisted. I could tell he was regaining his old self as he munched on biscuits and silently berated his bad behavior.

'I can believe this one,' our cousin gestured at me, and I tried to appear offended. 'But you, Enoch? How did he manage to get you into this mess?'

Before I could protest, Enoch came to my defense. 'It was Ben, the friend you recommended as I recall.'

'Ha! And so he was,' Nathan conceded as he held the fresh pitcher forth for my poor suffering brother.

'We were protesting the fare of the dining hall,' I added.

'Ah, so that was you,' Nathan murmured, his grin fading.

'Were we in the wrong? Should we not stand up for ourselves?'

Our older cousin pinned us with his gaze before responding. 'You should always stand up - for yourselves but especially for others. What you should not do is recklessly damage property that does not belong to you.'

Suddenly, I recalled that we had thrown those rocks.

'Damages that will be charged to the account which your father pays out of his own hard-earned farm profits.'

I was ashamed and could only imagine how Enoch felt. He would say we had broken the fifth commandment, failing to honor our father with our actions. His eyes were glassy now, not from drink, but from tears, and I made myself look away.

'Forgive us, cousin,' I murmured, wishing I could say as much to our father.

'Of course, I do,' Nathan said kindly, reprimand complete. 'Each of us makes mistakes when we are on our own for the first time. Let this be one you brothers learn a lesson from.'

We mumbled our shamefaced agreement, and Nathan nodded his approval. 'Off to class with you then. Might want to take a few of those in your pocket,' he said with a gesture toward the remaining biscuits. He left, waving off our murmured thanks.

Enoch clumsily rushed to pull on his clothes and gather his books. I knew we risked tardiness, but I put a hand on his arm.

'Brother, I owe you an apology. You would never have participated in such actions, had I not done so myself.'

He shook me off. 'It is I who am the older brother, and I should have set things to right.'

I pressed my lips together, not sure how I could keep him from taking all the blame onto himself. Instead, I followed his lead, as I should have done the previous evening, and readied myself for my lessons.

My head was down as we closed the door behind us, and I felt Enoch now reach for my arm.

'Nathan,' he started, closing his eyes to better form his words. 'That was prideful of me. I accept your apology and ask the same of you.'

I grinned, this more healing to me than water or biscuits had been. 'Thank you, brother. Now, we best not tarry.'

He smiled, nodded, and broke into a run toward his first class.

Ben later offered his apologies and forgiveness as well, and together we vowed to be young men that Linonia could be proud to call members. Enoch and I tackled the difficult task of writing to our father, confessing that we were both out of cash and had incurred an additional billing with the school. Cousin Nathan reassured us that father would be as understanding - this once - as he had been.

That accomplished and sent, we sat back, ready for a quieter, more relaxing evening than the one before. The fire crackled and we worked on the next day's lessons. Before long, Ben brought forth a new stack of broadsheets.

'What news?' I asked without reaching for them. I trusted Ben to share the most vital information and knew he would have already perused the newspapers.

'The *Boston Gazette* has a memorial for the anniversary of the Massacre.'

I reached for this, still uncertain in my own mind what had truly occurred that day. Whether a riot or a firing line, surely the British regulars had such an advantage against civilians that they also should have employed greater self-control. I heard Isaac *harrumph* from where he was sprawled on his bed. He had never needed to know more about the bloody event.

'Is the only news that of the last year?' Enoch inquired. 'Has the rebellion cooled?'

Another disgusted sound from Isaac.

I heard the hope in my brother's voice and couldn't help

but share it. Wasn't reconciliation with the mother country a brighter hope than a fight? Of course, I could never say as much without sounding like a coward.

Ben looked thoughtful. 'It is a good question, Primus, but it may be too much to hope that men who have seen a glimmer of liberty might decide it is not worth grasping.'

'Of course, we should fight for independence!' Isaac interjected, jumping from his bed. He looked at us in wonder. 'How can you even doubt it?'

Unfazed, Ben lowered the broadsheet in his hands. 'It is a question that requires more than fiery spirit, my friend. Should we not carefully consider a step such as civil war, a decision that will affect everyone living in the American colonies?'

Isaac shook his head angrily and stalked out the door, slamming it behind him. He was thinking that negotiations had been going on since we four were small children, and he wasn't wrong. But Ben wasn't wrong either. Going to war with the greatest military power in the world was not a decision to be made lightly. I felt a weight in my gut and worried for our future.

Elihu entered the room seconds after Isaac had left it. His raised brows informed us that he had seen our angry roommate in the hall and inquired what had occurred. Ben tossed some broadsheets his way.

'Perhaps we should discuss it at Linonia among calmer heads,' Enoch suggested.

Ben and I agreed that it was an appropriate question for the next time one of us had a turn to propose the topic.

Before that could happen, however, others ahead of us offered topics in the areas of mathematics and science that were interesting but difficult to be passionate about, at least for me. There were other exciting developments. We decided as a group to begin our own library to supplement the school library that did not always carry the titles we wished to read, and I was elected Linonia's scribe.

'That penmanship has paid off after all,' Isaac teased.

'So it has,' I agreed with a laugh. He could joke all he liked, but it was my pen that would create the permanent record of our meetings for the next term. I could imagine future Yale students flipping through the pages and noticing my name at the bottom of each entry.

'Should we admire Cato as a hero?'

The question hung in the air for a moment as we Linonians considered our position. The obvious answer was that we all admired Cato in Joseph Addison's tragedy, but could we defend this position? I pondered what characteristics of his were not admirable after I had recorded the question in our meeting minutes.

'Cato reminds us that there is a higher purpose than our personal desires,' James pointed out. 'Liberty and honor are preferable over life itself.'

'Even at the loss of his own son, Cato praises it as a beautiful death earned by virtue,' another added.

Here Enoch interjected. 'Marcus died nobly in battle, however, Cato did not. Was his death virtuous?'

I pressed my lips together to keep from being the one to agree with my brother, but Ben spoke up.

'Far from it, I would agree, my friend. Death by suicide goes against the law of God.'

'But not the gods of the Romans,' James countered. 'Cato believed it was more honorable to kill himself than be taken into custody by Caesar. He is not the only Roman to have performed what was believed to have been an honorable suicide.'

Now I could speak my mind without sounding like I was Enoch's mouthpiece. 'By which standard of virtue should we judge Cato, our own or his? Can we disdain a man of his time for doing what he believed was right? Might future generations take issue with some of our beliefs?'

James laughed. 'I see you have inherited Tallmadge's habit of asking more questions than you answer.'

Ben winked, and I felt my face warm.

'Secundus is right. We cannot judge a man who lived centuries earlier by the laws to which we hold ourselves. If his manner of death is our only objection, should we not rather focus on the virtue achieved during his life?'

I tipped my head to Stephen, who had supported my position. He was a year or two older, but he never disparaged the younger students.

'Well said, Hempstead,' said James. 'Has anyone further discourse?'

We each looked around, but I took some pride in the fact that those who had not yet spoken seemed reluctant to do so. I hoped it was because I had asked questions which required more than a moment to think. Perhaps we would all go to our bunks this night pondering what made an honorable death.

# Chapter 6
# Yale – August 1771

*The true christian self-denial is to give up ourselves; not only to bear some hard things, and deny some worldly pleasures, which may be done on lucrative principles, in expectation of a future repayment; but to give up our whole selves, and willingly become nothing that God may be all in all.*
- Nathan Strong

A bell clanged in my head, and I groaned sleepily, pulling my quilt up to block it out. My mind was in a fog and I was struggling to think of what day it was when Isaac snatched away my warm covers.

'That's the chapel bell, Secundus. You're usually awake by now.'

All I could do was groan.

Enoch's voice broke through the cloud that seemed to envelop me. 'Don't tarry, Nathan. We've a full day and so it must begin.'

Even in my groggy state, I discerned that my brother also sounded under the weather. That spurred me awake more than the chapel bell could. I forced my eyes open a slit, and even the low embers of our hearth seemed too bright. Enoch's cheeks were red as apples and his eyes were glassy. I wondered if my appearance matched his.

Of course, being young men, we could never admit such a weakness, especially not just as we started our third-year term. So, I followed my brother's lead and thrust away the comforting blankets.

I did not take my normal care with dressing and my hair stood on end, but I was soon joining my fellow students as we shuffled through the pale, chilly dawn to the campus chapel. We seemed to solemnly prepare ourselves for service, so quiet were we that the loudest sound was our feet crunching along the gravel path. In truth, we were barely awake and would be boisterous enough later on. A few coughed or sneezed, but none spoke.

The chapel was built of the same red brick that formed the walls of our dormitory, and it was of equal height, excepting the clock and bell tower that rose high above its surroundings. The minute hand of the clock pointed almost precisely upward, while the hour hand stretched in the opposite direction, seeming to give us the same option the preacher would soon offer: heaven or hell.

We moved faster as the bells began to strike the final call to worship. None wished to be the last to his seat or to fail to reach it before the final note echoed across the countryside. Swift was the earthly punishment for lack of reverence, and we could only imagine that God would be even less pleased.

As I slid into the pew beside my brother, I saw my worry mirrored in his countenance. I must share his feverish glow. He quickly looked away, clearly not wishing to give voice to concerns of illness that had potential to keep us from our lessons. We had not time to speak of it at any rate. As soon as we were settled into our places, the opening hymn began.

I moved my lips more than sang, my throat sore and my body weary. Enoch made more of an effort, but he was uncharacteristically out of tune. I refused to look his way. The unforgiving wooden bench felt more uncomfortable than usual, and Elihu glared at me when I squirmed too much for his taste.

It being a weekday, the service was brief, and God forgive me for being thankful that it wasn't the sabbath. By the time we were filing outside, my head throbbed and all I desired was to return to bed.

'Aren't you breaking your fast?' Isaac asked as I moved toward our room rather than the dining hall.

I hadn't even considered it, but my stomach protested at the thought. 'I'm just going to have a bit of a lie down,' I said.

Enoch nodded his head in agreement, following me. Isaac shrugged and took his separate way.

Upon entering our room, Enoch put a hand to my forehead and frowned in confirmation. 'You've a fever, and I'm certain that I must as well.'

I nodded, not needing to feel his damp, hot skin to know it to be true.

'I'm going back to bed,' I moaned as Enoch started sorting through books and papers. 'You're not going to class, are you?'

His shoulders sagged and he looked helplessly at me. 'How can we afford to miss?'

I shared his concern but could not keep my eyes open. The thought of standing, walking to class, and listening to a lecture sent a shiver of nerves through me. 'I cannot, Enoch.'

He hung his head, dropped the papers onto the desk, and tumbled into bed. I could only assume that sleep overtook him as quickly as it had myself.


'It is measles,' the doctor declared, standing abruptly as if eager to put distance between himself and our disease. He leaned closer to a female servant, who had been brought on campus to cope with the dozen young men suddenly bedridden. 'You can tell by the white spots in their throats, accompanied by fever and sensitivity to light. They will also begin to break out in a rash.'

'Yes, doctor,' she replied in the tone of one who is being

educated on a topic with which they are well acquainted.

'These rooms must be kept dark and warm. Therefore, the fires must be kept low, and you will have to supplement that heat with warm bricks under their blankets.'

'Yes, doctor.'

I heard their footsteps retreating and soon fell into a restless sleep plagued with thirst and troubled dreams.

I woke to Eliza mopping my brow with a cool cloth, but I could not make out her features in the dark room. My heart leapt, and I realized I had missed my sister more than I could ever confess.

'Eliza,' I said, though I scarcely recognized my own voice in the raspy utterance.

An unfamiliar voice responded, 'No, sir. I am Mary.'

The disappointment that assailed me shocked me with its ferocity. I felt like a small boy, despite my sixteen years, and wanted to be home more than I had during my entire time at Yale. I was horrified to feel a tear slip down my cheek and thankful for the darkness.

'Is Eliza your sweetheart?' Mary asked, and I could only shake my head in response. 'A sister then,' she guessed with the wisdom of a caregiver who has been in this situation enough to know who a young man is likely to desire near in his needful hours.

'Yes,' I rasped, 'and my brother, Enoch, is across the room . . . or at least he was.' I attempted to peer into the darkness as fear settled in my chest that he might also disappear.

'He is,' she reassured me, 'and he is recovering well, as are you.'

'Thanks to God, that is a blessing,' I murmured, already weary of talking. I closed my eyes, thinking I would go back to sleep, but Mary was not finished with her ministrations.

'Take some broth,' she encouraged, holding a steaming cup near my mouth. 'It will soothe that sore throat.'

Hunger pangs surprised me, and my throat did feel swollen and raw. I took a few sips before I settled into the pillows that propped me up and fell into an exhausted slumber once more.

When next I woke, Mary was gone and our cousin, Nathan, sat between the beds where Enoch and I battled with illness. He was humming an unfamiliar but soothing tune, so I didn't speak until he fell quiet.

My voice remained hoarse and unrecognizable. 'What is that song?'

'You are awake,' Nathan praised as if it were an amazing accomplishment. 'Let me fetch the broth.'

He was back before I could blink with a warm mug, and I was helped to sit up with pillows behind me. Once I had swallowed enough to please him, Nathan returned to my inquiry.

'It is a hymn that I am writing.'

I wished I could say everything that I was thinking – that it was a beautiful song, that I didn't realize he had such talent, that God would surely be pleased by his offering – but my throat was so sore. I nodded, and Nathan brought the mug to my mouth again.

'In fact, on that topic,' he began as he set aside the empty mug, 'I have something to share with you.'

'Yes?' I prodded when he seemed reluctant.

Meeting my eye, he admitted, 'I will be leaving Yale at the end of the term. I am going to complete my ministry licensing.'

My grin stretched wide and, I hoped, made up for my lack of words of congratulations. 'That is wonderful, cousin,' I managed to croak. Part of me did not want him to leave. He was a familiar, comforting familial presence here at college, but I would not deny him his future. 'Enoch will be eager to hear of your adventures.' I gestured toward my sleeping brother, and Nathan understood my unspoken question.

'He is well and was awake not long ago.' Then he spread his hands to encompass the entire building. 'Every student who has not previously suffered this malady is abed now.'

It was difficult to feel concern for my fellow man's suffering as weary and aching as I was. Nathan was talking about when he had the measles some years ago and how it enabled him to assist the servants without fear of infection. It also meant he knew just what to do to make Enoch and I comfortable now, and I thanked him as he replaced the cooled brick in my bedding with a hot one and handed me a mug of weak ale for sipping.

Days passed, and I knew not how many. Nathan or Mary was often at my bedside when I woke or arrived shortly as if they could sense a patient in need. It was not until later that I understood or appreciated the burden they bore during those weeks.

When Enoch and I finally rose from our beds to begin the challenge of catching up in our classes, we discovered that this task would not be as difficult as anticipated. Our entire class - ninety of us - had been bedridden for varied periods over the past few weeks. Therefore, it was our professors who were burdened with getting us all to the same point and determining what could be transitioned from required to recommended reading in order to finish the term on schedule.

We also realized that poor Mary and Nathan had been caring for us all with only intermittent guidance from the visiting physician. Our cousin had never complained or allowed his weariness to show. He would do well in the ministry.

I tired more quickly than before, as did my classmates,

leaving us little energy for hijinks of any sort. All our strength was reserved for our studies in a way that our professors would almost certainly have suggested we should always employ.

We were in our room, trying to study against the wishes of our weary bodies. My eyes kept drifting shut, and my book had been open to the same page for quite some time. Ben strolled in, stirring me awake and giving me an excuse to thankfully close the tome.

He, somehow, appeared unaffected by the illness that I knew had struck him down just as it had the rest of us. Where I was haggard with dark smudges under my eyes, Ben was fit and alert.

'What say you, Secundus?' he asked as he flopped onto my bed.

I rubbed my face wearily and asked, 'About what?'

'Shots fired.'

I was immediately alert. 'Shots? Where?' I felt bile rise in my throat at the thought of more violence. Had we truly believed the deaths in Boston would not lead to more?

'North Carolina.' He pulled a wrinkled broadsheet from his waistcoat and held it up. 'From my father.'

'Go on then.'

He read, and I imagined the landscape, though I didn't know if North Carolina looked as much like Connecticut as I was envisioning.

'Royal Governor Tyron marched a thousand militia against twice that many men of western Carolina calling themselves Regulators. They refused to pay fees and taxes while protesting government corruption and fraud.'

Ben trailed off and he scanned the broadsheet for the result of the clash.

'The militia overpowered the local rebels, claiming victory at Alamance, and hanged seven for treason.'

'Treason? Killed for protesting against corruption?' Enoch asked in a childlike and still slightly raspy voice.

My chest tightened, but I wasn't sure what I was feeling. Ben and I looked at each other, and I could tell the news disturbed him as well.

'All the way back in May,' I murmured, somewhat in awe that we had not heard sooner. 'The news certainly did not travel as it did after the Boston Massacre.'

Debates over that event aside, we referred to it now as it had become known.

'They had no Sam Adams in North Carolina to stir up the people, and no Paul Revere to capture the image for all to see,' said Ben.

'And no British regulars to blame,' I said, feeling this was the deeper reason for keeping the Battle of Alamance out of the broadsheets. Ben was nodding, so I added, 'They may have been serving the king just as the same, but few would be encouraged by the news of the North Carolina militia defeating a band of so-called rebels fighting for the same reasons for which we have been applauding those in Boston.'

'Governor Tyron pardoned those who took a pledge of allegiance to the crown,' Ben was reading again. 'Would you take it?' he asked, laying the sheet aside.

I took a deep breath. It was easy to quickly claim one's pledge to the cause of liberty, but could I remain steadfast with my life on the line? Seven men had been executed for treason by Governor Tyron. What would I do given the choice between betraying my ideals and losing my life?

'I would not,' Ben stated firmly, clearly believing I was

considering the question too long. Yet, I had no rebuke for him and knew he had not made the statement lightly.

'I believe you, and I hope that I would have the strength to do the same.'

# Chapter 7
# New Haven – July 1772

*He who fears death will never do anything worthy of a man who is alive.* - Seneca

I had spent little time over the past three years away from Yale's brick buildings, so when Isaac suggested a visit to the harbor I immediately joined him. New Haven was much larger than Coventry, but it was no longer intimidating. The proprietors and residents were just as friendly, only there were many times more of them.

On our way to the waterfront, Isaac and I detoured into several establishments, enjoying the balmy summer day and the freedom of putting space between us and our professors.

Dust hung low over the street like fog as many feet moved along to and fro and the occasional horse and rider sent up larger clouds. In contrast, the sun shone brightly over the harbor with the waves sparkling like flickering diamonds. Seagulls cried overhead as they swooped and soared, watching for fish close to the water's surface.

I felt my cheeks already turning pink under the sun's rays. It was a curse of my fair coloring, my mother had always said, that my skin burnt and peeled while some of my siblings turned a pleasing golden bronze in the summer. Were she at my side rather than in heaven, mother would have reprimanded me for not wearing a hat.

Isaac pulled at my sleeve, regaining my attention and directing me inside a store. I followed him and was ambushed by a cacophony of scents as the door shut behind me. A large man stood behind the counter of what appeared to be an apothecary shop.

'Afternoon, boys,' the proprietor boomed in greeting. 'What trouble you up to today?' He grinned, putting us at our ease.

'We would like some candied ginger, sir,' Isaac said, stepping forward. 'Do you have any?'

'Do I have any?' The man shook his head as if it were an insult as he took out a small square of paper. 'Do you have the penny?' he asked with an upraised brow, pretending to withhold the treat from us.

Isaac grinned and placed the coin on the counter. 'Thank you, Mr Arnold,' he said, taking the twist of paper from him.

Mr Arnold laughed jovially as he scooped up Isaac's penny and waved us out of his store. We nodded our thanks and stepped back out into the sunshine and salt-scented breeze.

I breathed deeply, attempting to rid my lungs of the thick fragrance of the apothecary shop. Isaac swiftly untwisted the paper and handed me a generous portion of candied ginger. It was sweet and tangy on my tongue, like the summer version of Christmas gingerbread cookies.

We walked down to the waterfront where Isaac used another coin to procure access to a sailboat for the afternoon. The warm breeze billowed the sails, and the waves made a mildly soothing rhythm against the hull. In only a few minutes, we were away from shore, basking in the sun and sensation of independence.

Isaac and I had spoken little when I noticed a dark tinge to the horizon, and I pointed it out to my friend. He shrugged nonchalantly, but I noticed that he turned the sailboat toward shore.

'Is it a storm?' I asked, he being the more experienced sailor.

Isaac peered in the direction of the dark clouds, but I was uncertain if he wished to delay his response or if he were trying to gauge the danger they posed.

'Could be,' he finally said. 'Best if we don't tarry.'

Compared to his typical lighthearted irreverence, this was a serious warning. I gazed out to sea and could see that the dark clouds had come closer with astonishing speed. Fine hairs stood on my arm as a cool wind caught in our sails and Isaac adjusted our course.

I was no help to him. He urged the boat to return to shore, but the storm clouds were faster, whipping the waves into a foam and blotting out the sun. I prayed under my breath and watched the world around us transition from sunny day to dark tempest.

Lightning streaked across the sky just as thunder boomed all around our little boat. I knew it to be early afternoon, but the sky gave the appearance of dusk as fat raindrops soaked us as soon as they began to fall.

'Isaac! What can I do?' I asked. I was forced to shout over the crashing of waves, rolling thunder, and splatter of rain.

He shrugged and tried not to let me see his fear.

'Pray we don't drown, Secundus' he ordered with a wink, not taking his hands from the ropes and rudder.

My lack of fear surprised me. I knew how to swim, had done so in Coventry's great pond since I could toddle down to its sandy shore, but I had no confidence that I could make my way back to New Haven should our sailboat become overwhelmed. Was my guardian angel calming my nerves, or was I arrogant in thinking I was omnipotent?

The boardwalk came into view, and Isaac and I grinned at each other through the pelting rain. A large wave set the boat on its side, and our grins evaporated as we hovered at the tipping point, wondering if it would remain upright or capsize. Lightning flashed, rain poured, and thunder rolled through my very bones.

Then the boat slammed down into the valley between towering waves, and we laughed our fear away. We were now close enough to shore that we told ourselves we could reach it, even if our boat did not. That may not have been true, but the lie gave us comfort as it floated wordlessly between us.

We weren't as terrified the next time the boat hung on a wave, balanced precariously on its side. I held my breath only a second as we waited for it to crash down briefly before rising on the next crest.

My hair was plastered to my head, and I blinked to clear raindrops from blurring my vision. I could see the dock clearly now. The owner of our boat waved as he stood there, heedless of the surf and rain which both soaked him in equal measure. I waved back, to let him know I could see him and ease his concerns about his boat.

The muscles in Isaac's arms strained against his wet shirt as he wrestled the sailboat toward the dock. A vein pulsed close to the surface in his neck, and I dared not let on that I could discern his anxiety was greater than he would ever admit. He caught my gaze and smirked nonchalantly.

'Almost there now, Secundus. You won't drown.'

'I'll never drown,' I shouted back, the words coming almost of their own accord, and I wondered why I had said them.

Isaac gave me a brief bemused look before the sailboat demanded his attention.

The storm thundered around us as we finally reached the dock and the sailboat's owner relieved Isaac of duty, securing the boat to the dock with thick ropes. We climbed out, laughing as only young men who have escaped an encounter with death can. Finally, we skidded across the wet dock and placed our feet on solid ground.

Away from any who might overhear us, Isaac asked me if I had been afraid to drown.

'I will never be drowned. I am to be hanged.'

I had spoken again without thinking and paused upon seeing Isaac's stricken expression.

'What do you mean?' he said in a voice scarcely above a whisper and far too serious for the likes of him.

'Nothing,' I murmured, wishing I hadn't uttered it. 'Nothing but an old joke.'

I tried to stalk away, but Isaac caught my arm. The rain was lighter now, and the sun peeked through breaks in the clouds. I was surprised at his concern.

'It's nothing, really,' I insisted with an unconvincing laugh. 'The other boys teased me,' I began, not really wanting to explain. 'I have a birthmark.' My hand went to the nape of my neck. I couldn't feel the mark, but I knew it was there. Voices of children echoed in my mind, telling me that the hangman would be my doom. I was cursed with a witch's mark that told me how I would die.

His mood changed as quickly as the weather, and Isaac laughed, slapping my arm and shaking his head.

'You had me worried! Made me think you had foreseen your own fate, for heaven's sake!'

He walked on ahead of me, toward the warmth of our hearth in Connecticut Hall, but now it was I who felt the chill of foreboding even more than when I thought we might have been lost at sea.

# Chapter 8
# Yale – December 1772

*I distinguish greatly between a King and a Tyrant, a King is the guardian and trustee of the rights and Laws of the people but a Tyrant destroys them.* – Reverend John Allen

Snow carpeted campus, creating an immaculate landscape with the pure white dramatically contrasting with the red brick of our Connecticut Hall. It was not yet as terribly cold as it would be in a few weeks, so we had decided to go outside and stretch our limbs, which were stiff from hours hunched over our desks.

'Shall we walk down to the waterfront?' Isaac asked. He was ever attracted to the water, even when it was a rough, frigid foam. Lakes and ponds were frozen, but the Long Island Sound moved too swiftly with the currents of the Atlantic Ocean for ice to form.

Enoch was protesting Isaac's suggestion but offering none of his own. Ben and I were content to shuffle through the snow, creating paths to nowhere and kicking icy fluff at each other.

'Have you heard from cousin Nathan?' Ben asked.

I nodded. 'He prepares for his preaching license.' Ben only nodded as he kicked snow into a pile. It made me think of snow forts that Enoch and I used to build. 'Do you consider the ministry yourself?' I asked. 'Following in your father's footsteps?'

Ben shrugged and laughed lightly. 'He would like that, but, no, I do not think so. I will take a teaching position, unless fighting begins.'

I felt a shiver that had naught to do with the cold. 'You will join the militia?' I imagined Ben in uniform, injured, dying. What a waste of his brilliant mind that would be.

'If it comes to that,' Ben agreed. 'If not us, Secundus, who will step forward and defend our country - our homes?'

Here am I, send me. If Enoch were more revolution minded, he might have mentioned Isaiah's words and eagerness to serve his Lord as recorded in scripture. I kept them to myself, unsure if I would have the courage to say them and ashamed by my hope that it would not become necessary.

'Hey!' my brother shouted, breaking my reverie.

'Look sharp, Primus!'

Isaac was laughing and my brother was brushing snow from his face. Our mischievous friend had rolled a supply of snowballs while we had been lost in conversation, and he now pelted us without mercy. We ran for cover, each man for himself, and tried to mold ammunition of our own as Isaac pressed his advantage.

It did not last long. We were less appealing targets when harder to hit, and our fingers became red and numb. Enoch was the first to surrender, holding his hands in the air and pleading that we fetch warm milk from the dining hall before camping out in front of our hearth.

'I second the motion,' I shouted, leaving my hiding spot with raised hands.

'Ha! You would, Secundus,' Isaac laughed.

I shrugged at Enoch. It was the first time I recalled the nickname feeling like an insult, but I knew Isaac meant nothing by it.

Ben also emerged, looking as though none of us had struck him. He said nothing but started walking toward the hall and we all followed.

We gratefully accepted mugs of warm milk from the cook and wrapped our cold hands around them. After defrosting for a bit, we agreed to meet back in our room.

'You stoke the fire,' Ben commanded, 'and I will fetch some things from my room.'

We momentarily parted ways and had the room warm by the time Ben rejoined us.

'My father has sent a sermon for our Christmas reading.' Ben entered the room with a lopsided grin and his arms full of packages wrapped in brown paper.

'Oh, what have you there, Tallmadge?' Isaac perked up. 'It appears you have offerings more interesting than your father's latest sermon.'

Ben laughed as he deposited his load onto my bed. 'It is not my father's sermon. It is from the Reverend John Allen of Boston. He gave an oration on the spirit of liberty that my father thought would be of interest to us.'

Isaac remained unimpressed, but I moved forward to accept the pamphlet in Ben's hand.

'You have read it,' I stated rather than asked, and Ben nodded, indicating he would remain silent until I had time to peruse the oration myself. 'He responds to the *Gaspee* affair.' I looked up for confirmation.

'He does,' Ben stated, and Isaac's interest was revived.

'Why didn't you say so?' He exclaimed, as if word of current events was more important to attend to than the Word of God.

I spoke as I read. 'He states that forcing men to be tried in England goes against their rights as Englishmen.'

'Tis impossible for that to include a jury of their peers,' Ben agreed.

'Are they not accused of treason?' Enoch asked. 'Might we expect a trial for treason to be held in the mother land?'

We each might have reacted in anger if we did not know

Enoch and understand that his inquiry did not evince a lack of passion for liberty.

'But was it treason?' Ben asked.

Enoch blinked as if it had not occurred to him to question the charge itself, so Ben continued.

'Setting fire to the *Gaspee* should be considered an act of piracy, not rebellion.'

'But it was a Royal Navy ship,' Enoch pointed out, 'not a mere merchant vessel.'

'The men were not organized against the king,' Isaac pointed out. 'It was a raid, as Ben has said, piracy. Would any but an American be charged with treason after such an event?'

Enoch frowned and nodded as he considered this.

'It is my understanding that they are not even certain which men were part of the attack,' I added as I continued to scan John Allen's pamphlet. 'What of an innocent man forced to sacrifice months of his life and livelihood to participate in such a trial?'

Enoch murmured his agreement.

'It is not their fault the Brits couldn't manage the river without getting stuck,' Isaac added with a smirk. 'I could steer a schooner with greater success than that Navy crew.'

We laughed and nodded our agreement. I, for one, put great faith in Isaac's ability as a seaman since our sailing incident.

But Enoch had not yet made up his mind. 'Was it not an act of war? Were they stealing goods, if they were pirates? Or were they traitors acting against the king as charged?'

This made us all pause, for it did seem to be an act of war, but we were not at war. Not officially. Would that be the result of this growing division? I tried to imagine what civil war would look like, but I could not fathom it.

'Still,' Ben broke into our private thoughts. 'Whether

pirates or traitors, their trial rightly belongs on the side of the ocean upon which their crime took place. No man has a jury of their peers three thousand miles from their home.'

I returned to the pamphlet and found that Reverend Allen agreed wholeheartedly with my friend. 'He calls it more than an infringement of liberty,' I read aloud. 'He accuses the Royal Governor of "cruelty, injustice, and barbarity." More than that, he insists that the king is a trustee of authority, and that given by the people.'

I looked up to gauge the reaction of my friends. This was not the way people had talked about the king when I was growing up. Did they find it as controversial as it seemed to me?

Enoch's eyes were wide, but his brow was furrowed in thought. Yes, my brother would be of one mind with myself. Isaac's smirk remained. He was one that thrived on this recent change of point of view – that the power was in the hands of the people rather than a monarch. Ben remained inscrutable. Thoughtful.

I was surprised when Enoch spoke. 'Do kings receive their authority from God, as has been long understood, or do they receive it from the people whom they govern, as men like this Reverend Allen say today?'

'It is worth pondering,' Ben agreed noncommittally.

'Allen includes the example of King Charles being removed by the people,' I said, holding the pamphlet out to my brother. 'What think you of that?'

Ben spoke before Enoch had the chance. 'It is a bold, almost threatening statement. The preacher may find himself on a ship headed for his own treason trial.'

He had said it lightly, but not one of us laughed.

# Chapter 9
# Yale – July 1773

*It would be an honor for me to die in his place.* – Pythias

'Ben has written,' I announced as I stepped through the door. I held the missive up as if I believed Enoch would request proof of my statement. 'It is so odd that he is not just down the hall.'

'And peaceful....and free of mischief.'

I grinned, knowing Enoch missed Ben just as I did, even if he still rankled over the trouble he had often encouraged. 'You know as well as I that Ben was just as often a good influence, spurring on discussion and sharing broadsheets. Would we be as well informed had we not shared our collegiate days with him?'

My grin faded as my own statement brought home the fact that those days were truly over. Ben wrote from Wethersfield, where he had accepted a teaching position. I would forge a similar path after commencement. Overachiever that he was, Ben was already gone, and Yale was not the same place without him.

'True,' Enoch grudgingly conceded. 'What news does he share?' In spite of himself, my brother stretched his neck to see over my shoulder. 'He writes you again as Damon.'

'Damon to my Pythias,' I murmured, skimming the text for important news.

'You and your Cicero,' Enoch mumbled, and I wondered if I heard a hint of jealousy in his voice.

I turned to him, lowering the letter. 'Damon and Pythias were friends, willing to lay down their lives for each other, just as patriots shall be asked to do if events turn toward independence.'

'I know who they are,' Enoch snapped. Then he seemed to regret his sharp tone. 'What has Damon to share?'

'He uses far more words than necessary to imply loneliness and lack of fulfillment in his post.'

I tried to imagine teaching children their letters rather than discussing philosophy with my fellow Linonians, and the weight in my gut increased. Was this the future for which we must settle? Enoch only grunted. He would eventually secure a position as the shepherd of a congregation, so he couldn't fully appreciate the dullness of teaching. Yet, Ben and I shared higher hopes.

'He hints at a lady friend and asks that I remind you also to write.'

'That is all? Nothing of politics?' Enoch did not bother to hide his disappointment. Superfluous words of intimate friendship were in no short supply. He desired news of the outside world.

'Not this time,' I admitted, a bit disappointed myself.

'Pythias stood up to a tyrant,' Enoch reminded me unnecessarily. Ben had not written of revolution, but his choice of pen names kept independence at the forefront of our minds, nonetheless.

Though I wished to involve myself in more important events, the practical side of me settled for inquiring of those who, like Ben, had already pursued employment in teaching. If I, for now, must take on a schoolroom, I would make the best of it that I could and aim to make my pupils eager learners.

I wrote letters and asked questions, keeping my own list of advice and ideas for use in the schoolhouse. One topic intrigued me above others, and I was pleased to see it would be the subject of a debate during commencement exercises.

'The education of women?' Enoch raised that brow at me once again. 'You will speak in favor?'

'Of course,' I stated firmly, standing a bit taller than I had before. 'And why not?'

Enoch only laughed and waved me away. He would not be dragged into the debate. 'I shall leave that for your opponent.'

He moved to return to his packing, for we would soon leave this home of four years, but I refused to drop the subject so easily.

'Can you not imagine Eliza's joy had she been able to study with Dr Huntington as we did? Remember how she would ask almost daily about our lessons even as she learned her own skills under our mother's tutelage?'

Enoch nodded thoughtfully, neither supporting nor countering these questions. 'It is an interesting idea, and I look forward to the debate,' was all he would commit.

I had plans that went well beyond an academic debate. These plans I did not share with anyone, not even Enoch, just yet. I would indeed be well prepared for the upcoming debate.

# Chapter 10
# Yale – September 1773

*We have lived together, not as fellow students and members of the same college but as brothers and children of the same family. –* Nathan Hale

The day of our commencement had arrived, and I was equal parts sorrowful and tingling with anticipation. My Yale dorm room felt more like home to me than my father's house, but I would soon be leaving it. Not only that, Enoch and I would go our separate ways, and I dreaded the thought of losing my constant companion. Not that I could ever admit such a thing, of course.

As my cousin, Nathan Strong, had at his commencement exercises four years earlier, I dressed in homespun. If anything, the passion for domestic goods had only increased and the relations between we colonies and our king devolved, but that was a thought for another day. Eliza had sewed the suit with her own caring hands, and it was cut perfectly for my frame using measurements I had sent. I was eager to see her again.

My hair was tied into a neat queue and my face clean-shaven. I was vain enough to know my appearance was pleasing but humble enough to not speak this aloud. My grooming complete, I turned my thoughts to the debate in which I would soon participate. Mother would be proud, I think, could she be here, and I wondered if the Lord allowed mothers glimpses of their children from heaven.

When I stepped up to the podium, I felt both nervous and self-assured. My opponent appeared equally sure of his part, but this did not shake my confidence. Hours of Linonia debates and discussions had prepared me for this day. We had dug deeply into almost every subject imaginable. Oh, how I would miss those weekly dissertations.

The mediator stepped forward between we two debate participants.

'The next exercise shall be in the form of a debate between Mr Sampson and Mr Hale,' he nodded to us each in turn.' They shall discuss whether the education of daughters be not without any just reason more neglected than that of sons.'

Our audience was filled with reactions that revealed upon which side of this discussion each found themselves. Many older men, likely my classmates' fathers, looked smug and closed-minded, while their daughters sat forward eagerly. The mediator nodded to each of us, and we began.

My opponent was quick to start his oration, and I was content to allow him. I listened for points that I wished to counter when my own turn came.

'The education of daughters is by no means neglected, though it differs from that of sons. Sons, quite rightly, are educated in mathematics, history, philosophy, and the affairs of state and business. These subjects have no bearing on the daily life of women and are therefore not a part of their education. Girls have learned their domestic arts from their mothers and grandmothers since the beginning of time, and it is a system of education that provides each with the wisdom required for the efficient running of a household, the care and raising of children, and the fulfilling of wifely duties.'

I resisted the urge to roll my eyes and wondered if Mr Sampson had any sisters. However, some in the audience were grunting their approval and nodding at his sagacity.

'I agree that our sisters receive timeless wisdom from our mothers and grandmothers,' I began, putting my opponent at his ease. 'We would be unfortunate indeed if this wealth of knowledge were not passed down from generation to generation. My own grandmother could treat any illness or injury with herbs and potions, and my closest sister sewed with her own dear hands the fine suit in which I stand before you today.'

Those who had been pleased by my opponent's opening lines seemed even more satisfied now, and the women who had anticipated a speech in their support slumped back into their seats. But I was not finished.

'However,' I continued, gazing around the audience with what I hoped was a winning grin, 'why should our sisters be limited to these important skills?' I gestured to my opponent. 'You yourself likely learned from your father how to farm, how to hunt, and how to keep a ledger. Yet, you are here to deepen your wisdom through coursework that encourages you to think critically and broaden your horizons. Could not our sisters do the same? Why limit those who wish to learn based on something as arbitrary and unchosen for oneself as sex?'

One young woman gave four quick claps of applause before stilling herself. The young man across the platform from me cleared his throat and cast me a glance that informed me he was less than convinced.

'Mr Hale would have us believe that there are no differences between a man and a woman,' he exclaimed with a condescending chuckle at my expense. 'He has admitted that boys and girls are taught different vital skills at home, yet he wishes us to believe that both should attend a great school together,' his arms came up to envelope Yale's campus. 'Are we to believe that women can read and comprehend Plato or that they have the capacity for advanced calculations?' He laughed and shook his head.

I did not wait for him to continue. 'Of course women can comprehend Plato, and why not?' I directed my question to the young ladies in the audience who nodded eagerly in response. 'And should not the women who will become mothers of our children have the best education they can obtain? How can it but make them better stewards of the resources and young minds to which we entrust them?'

'Perhaps you would also suggest that women go into business or join the state assembly?' Samson jeered.

Some laughter greeted his question, but I was quick to respond.

'Perhaps they should!' I ignored the gasps and grumbles of anger. 'Who among us does not know a wife of finer mind than her husband?' I paused, trying to fix my gaze on those who appeared to be my biggest detractors. 'I have no reason to believe that a woman lacks the capacity to learn anything that can be learned by a man, if she is given the opportunity to do so. That they are denied that opportunity is neglect for the purpose of favoring sons.'

Samson was shaking his head as though I was the greatest idiot he had the misfortune of encountering, but the ladies in the audience beamed at me.

'I have no notion who shall care for children or the homestead in this vision of yours, Mr Hale. Do you suggest that you can improve upon the roles that God himself has assigned to each sex?'

I forced myself to remain calmer than my opponent as I responded. 'I am no heretic and have great respect for women's role as mothers, but do we answer the command to love our wives as Christ loved the church if we neglect their minds and limit their educations?' Before he could interrupt, I gestured toward my audience. 'What of women who are abused or abandoned? Should we not give them the ability to care for themselves? How much richer could our community be if we did not leave fallow the minds of half of our population?'

The mediator stepped forward to inform us that our time was running short. I tried to assess if I had changed the mind of any in the audience. It was difficult to tell, and I could only hope that I had planted seeds that might germinate and take hold. We each had one more opportunity to speak. Sampson drove home his point.

'As you know, Mr Hale, "a little learning is a dangerous thing." Shall we encourage revolution among the fair sex by educating them as though they were men?' He shook his head at this ridiculous thought. 'Women are not neglected in their education. It is only that they require a different education than that needed to be successful as a man. When men and women work together in the roles assigned to them by their Creator, there all happiness lies.'

I allowed him to receive his applause before making my final statement. I tried not to grin too broadly.

'You make my case for me, Mr Sampson. For when Mr Pope warns of a little learning he is warning us of inadequate education, just what you suggest for our sisters.' I thanked God once again for our Linonian debates, for Alexander Pope was fresh in my mind. 'Perhaps it is you, Mr Sampson, who needs to "drink deep or not taste the Pierian spring" for, in this case, "shallow draughts intoxicate the brain and drinking largely sobers us again." Those who think they know much but who truly know little are the most dangerous kind, as Mr Pope warns us. Complete ignorance is a safer state than insufficient wisdom. Therefore, let us not neglect the thorough education of our sisters and daughters.'

I could not discern if my applause was greater than that for my opponent, but I was content to see the encouraged faces of the young ladies who had listened. I prayed that they might use some of my arguments to improve their own futures. In that moment, I knew of another step I must take to help them. Before my thoughts could form any further, my arms were grasped in a firm grip and I was spun around to face Ben.

'Well done, Secundus!' he exclaimed. 'You've established your case well and made yourself a favorite among the young ladies.'

I laughed and felt my cheeks warm at his words. Of course, I had not participated in the debate to attract feminine attention, yet I could not say it was a detrimental consequence.

'Ben . . .' my words trailed off as I struggled with what to say. Men did not confess that they missed their friends, not aloud. I wanted to embrace him as a brother but settled for the firm handshake he offered.

'I was disappointed that Sampson did not offer the argument that too much education makes a lady unattractive,' Ben said with a laugh. 'How wonderful had you been able to gaze upon your chosen lady as you offered reassurance that learned women were quite beautiful.'

Enoch and Isaac had joined us, and they laughed uproariously at this suggestion.

'I can assure you that I have not set my eye on any lady.' I shrugged. 'After all, we each prepare to leave.'

Their laughter faded as if a dark cloud had covered us. Only Ben seemed unfazed. He slapped me on the back and led us away from where Sampson was being congratulated by a group of grateful fathers.

'You have secured a position?' Ben asked when we reached a quieter spot.

I nodded. 'The school at Haddam Landing. Enoch and I plan to spend some time with our uncle in New Hampshire before I make my way to my post. Uncle Samuel prepares collegiate hopefuls at his school in Portsmouth, and I thought he might offer useful advice.'

'Despite the fact that he attended Harvard,' Enoch added to the amusement of our little group.

I grinned and admitted that a debate on the qualities of the rival schools was an inevitable part of the visit. Also inescapable was the fact that Enoch and I would part ways when we left New Hampshire. I looked at him now, talking and laughing light-heartedly. An empty place was already forming inside me at the thought of our separation, but no one would discern it as I joked along with the others.

'How have you found your employment?' I asked of Ben, and the rest of us quieted to hear his response. He was the trailblazer among us having already spent the past semester teaching rather than taking lessons alongside us.

'It has been instructive and entertaining at times, but at others admittedly dull. Thankfully, the ladies of Wethersfield have welcomed me warmly and made up for any inadequacies of my pupils.'

I shook my head at how Ben could be the most intellectual among us while also giving the appearance of cool nonchalance. I, for one, knew that he likely spent many more evenings with his books than in female company. Still, it was encouraging to hear him speak of the schedule he kept and some teaching aids he preferred. The ease with which he spoke of his duties reassured me that I, too, would be equal to the task.

'Primus, you will return to your father's house?' Ben asked, and all eyes turned to my brother.

Enoch nodded, unashamed to confess that after four years of relative independence he returned to Coventry. 'The good reverend, Dr Huntington, has agreed to prepare me for my ministerial license. Nathan and I,' he nodded toward me, 'gained much under his tutelage before coming here, and I look forward to continuing my studies.'

'A preacher – our Primus! I can hardly credit it,' Ben said with a wink. His own father was a reverend, so Enoch knew it was only teasing. I wondered what it had been like to have a father like Ben's, not that I did not love my own.

Isaac also planned to accept a teaching position for the time being. I believed we all had loftier goals, but we had to make our start so teaching it was to be for us.

Our group was split up by parents coming to claim us. Our father greeted Enoch and I warmly but awkwardly. We were not the same boys that he had sent to school four years ago. I stood taller than our father, while Enoch looked at him eye to eye.

'Proud I am of you boys,' he said in a low rumble as he shook our hands and patted our arms.

'Thank you, sir,' Enoch and I said almost in unison, making us sound like the young boys he still expected us to be.

'Your ma . . . she'd have been proud of you, too.' He sniffled a bit, and I was touched that his emotions for our mother still rose so close to the surface this many years after her death. 'She always wanted you to go to Yale.' He nodded firmly, his duty to her complete.

# Chapter 11
# Coventry – October 1773

*The happiest moments of my life have been the few which I have passed at home in the bosom of my family.* - Thomas Jefferson

During the two day trip to Coventry, Enoch and I discovered a new companionship with our father. By the time we arrived at the homestead, he spoke to us as fellow men rather than the boys who had left four years earlier. Instead of instructing us, he asked Enoch questions of theology and inquired of my lesson plans. Still, I could tell that Enoch shared my apprehension regarding our status as outsiders in what used to be our home.

I caught Enoch's eye. Without speaking, I knew he understood. We would stay but a few days and then make our way to Uncle Samuel. He nodded, and I turned away.

One person at home I did look forward to seeing. Our sister, Eliza, was no longer the child who had packed our saddlebags before we left for Yale. In fact, in two short months she would be married, though she would still live in the village with her husband. Samuel Rose was a doctor who would provide her with a comfortable situation, and I hoped that she was also in love.

When we arrived at my father's homestead, Enoch and I were reminded that we were not the only ones who had changed over the course of the passing years. Richard was a strapping sixteen-year-old who I imagined was a great help to our aging father with the farm work. David and Billy were a young copy of Enoch and myself. At twelve and fourteen, they clearly shared a special bond. I wondered if they, too, would go to Yale together soon.

Little Joanna helped our stepmother in the kitchen the way Eliza used to assist our mother, and it made me wonder how much of her real mother Joanna remembered.

Besides Eliza, it was these younger siblings that occupied our attention. Our older brothers, Samuel and Joseph, were preoccupied with the running of the farms – our father's and one that Samuel had recently purchased – and had little time for congratulating the family collegiates.

Missing was my second oldest brother, John. He had been the first of us boys to marry, finding his wife conveniently at home in our stepmother's daughter, Sarah. They had set up their own household not many miles away.

The family room was full enough without the eldest three, and I enjoyed being warmly enveloped by the chaotic brood. A low fire sizzled, but it wasn't much necessary for warmth with so many bodies packed in and Eliza and our stepmother passing around hot rum punch. The younger boys moaned that theirs was too watered down, but our stepmother just smiled and Eliza smacked them lightly to send them on their way.

I was content to sit back and listen to the banter of my siblings and feel as though I was getting to know them anew. It couldn't have been more different from the evenings that Enoch and I had grown used to, pouring over our books or involved in erudite debate of our Linonia Society. I felt myself relax more than I had in ages and almost lulled off to sleep before I was called to attention.

'Nathan, are you looking forward to teaching?' Eliza asked, and I could tell by the light in her eyes that she wished such a door might be open to her.

On the other hand, I heard the voice of an unidentified younger brother mumble about just how boring it sounded.

I sat forward and shook myself awake a bit before responding. 'It is not what I hope to do as a career, but I and many of my fellow graduates find it a good stepping stone to something else.'

Enoch piped up and mentioned Ben. He still hoped that Ben would follow his father's footsteps and join Enoch in the ministry, but I had my doubts.

'I may strive toward the law.' I shrugged. 'Honestly, I wish I were more sure. This position will give me time to think on it.'

'My son a lawyer,' our father murmured, and I could hear the pride in his voice. He glanced at his wife, who had remained quietly at his side, and squeezed her hand. She smiled at him, and I wondered that we had been afraid she might run roughshod over his household.

'You shall already have a reverend,' Eliza scolded. 'Do not be too vain about the quality of your offspring.'

We laughed and all looked to Enoch who blushed predictably at being held up as the most admirable son of our father's large brood.

More hot rum went around, and the talk quieted as we each became sleepy and content. Our stepmother started shooing the younger ones off to bed, and Eliza promised a celebratory feast to break our fast in the morning. Enoch and I climbed the steps to our old room that we had been happily informed was restored to us for the length of our stay.

'What think you, Nathan? Does it feel strange to be back in this room?' Enoch asked as we climbed under the covers before the warmth of the rum and companionship could flee.

I sighed and considered this. 'It is strange to be home and no longer feel a child. I think it is that more than the changes we had feared.'

Enoch murmured a response that sounded like agreement, but he was already fading into slumber. I soon did the same.

The next morning, Eliza was in the kitchen, as promised, with warm blueberry muffins sprinkled with sugar, sizzling bacon and sausage, a basket of eggs, and a bubbling cauldron of hot chocolate. We eagerly tucked into our meal, glad to never again face the dining hall fare.

'Nathan, let us trace your profile into the door. It will give father something to remember you by.' Eliza was pointing at my shadow as she said this. The sunlight came through the windows at just the right angle to leave a fair silhouette, and she had already grabbed a bit of charcoal.

I shrugged and then remained perfectly still for Eliza to draw my outline on the kitchen's oak door. Once complete, I thought it looked rather flat and shapeless, but if it pleased her that was well enough.

'It is Enoch who shall miss me more than father,' I teased my brother to hide my own insecurity at our eminent parting.

Enoch only laughed and shook his head, and I knew he felt the same.

Eliza beamed at both of us. She was most pleased to have her closest brothers home, if only for a few days. After all, she would soon be keeping her own household as well.

I was a bit jealous that she and Enoch would have time together when he returned from our trip to Portsmouth, and I would be going to claim my position in Haddam Landing. I would never have confessed it, not even to my future preacher brother. It couldn't be helped, so I would choose to be happy for them.

For a moment, I wondered what my father thought of all these constant changes. What would it be like once the younger ones made their own way as several of us already had? It was difficult to imagine him here alone with my stepmother in this big empty house.

Our time in Coventry flew by, and before we knew it Enoch and I were packing our saddlebags for our trip to New Hampshire. Eliza, just as she had when we left for Yale, ensured that we were well-fed. Our fare was much finer than the bread and cheese she had provided us with all those years earlier, but I appreciated that the sentiment was the same. However far we went, we took our sister's love with us.

# Chapter 12
# Portsmouth – November 1773

*There is nothing more divine than education. It is only through education that one truly becomes man.* – Plato

It was with mixed feelings that Enoch and I left Coventry once again to pursue our plans to visit our relations in New Hampshire. Enoch had the benefit of knowing that he would return for his instruction under Reverend Huntington. I, however, was unsure when I would see my family again, and leaving, therefore, was bittersweet.

I enjoyed the sweet feeling of independence that greeted us along with the crisp autumn air, but I knew I would miss the company of my siblings and especially our father. Once again just the two of us, Enoch and I fell into our comfortable companionship on the road.

News had arrived of Britain's Tea Act, and it felt reminiscent of our Linonia meetings to discuss the potential impact of this action.

'I had allowed myself to believe we might reconcile,' Enoch admitted. 'There has been relative calm since the Boston Massacre.'

'Yet British regulars still roam the streets,' I countered.

Enoch nodded. 'Yes, I suppose it would be much more difficult to retain faith in a peaceful solution if one lived in Boston.'

'And now this act gives the East India Company a monopoly in the Americas. What if Parliament decides to give similar privileges to favored companies over other commodities?'

'They impose no new taxes but take control over American trade all the same.'

'How many good merchants will find themselves driven out of business? This could mean a complete loss of livelihood for countless men.'

'Perhaps you should pursue an apprenticeship to study law,' Enoch said with a grin. 'You debate these topics with greater skill than I.'

I laughed but briefly for the concern remained. 'What of those who depend upon trade?'

'Good that we have chosen different paths,' Enoch murmured, but I knew he did not mean that we should accept the tyrannical act, only that we should be thankful for God's protection of our own family.

'What acts of retribution will soon take place?' I wondered aloud.

Enoch shook his head and we fell into silence, each remembering Revere's engraving of the Boston Massacre.


Our uncle, Samuel Hale, lived in Portsmouth, and it struck me as odd to live so near a neighbor with no orchards and fields. Samuel was a lawyer and Latin school teacher, so he had no time for farming. Although I had spent my college years away from our father's farm, I somehow always envisioned myself owning one myself someday. Only recently, had I considered the idea that I might be better suited to a life more like Uncle Samuel's.

Enoch and I approached Samuel's home, murmuring a few comments about the beauty of the village with red brick and white clapboard houses against the backdrop of hills blanketed with forests on one side and the cerulean of the harbor on the other. A cold wind blew from the waterfront, through the streets and up into the trees, giving us a chill, but it must have been welcome in the summer months.

Along the way, we had talked about what we remembered about our uncle, but we had been young children when last we had visited with our father. I recalled that he had a son our age and wondered if he was yet under his father's roof.

A man who could only be our Uncle Samuel stepped out of a picturesque home with black shutters. The paint was snowy white and not peeling like that of many of his neighbors. Samuel himself was easy to identify even if my memory failed me, for he was a darker version of our father. His hair was deep auburn and his eyes hazel, but the way his welcoming smile made his eyes crinkle was so reminiscent of my father that I felt my heart strain in my chest.

'Enoch! Nathan!' he looked between us, and I doubted he knew which of us was which, but he held his arms wide, nonetheless. I had grown so used to being called Primus and Secundus that hearing our Christian names thus caught me somewhat off guard.

We dismounted and embraced him in turn, Enoch making a mundane remark that required using my name to clear up our uncle's uncertainty. The little habits he had for putting people at their ease would help make him a good preacher, I was sure.

Greetings complete, we turned to enter the house, and the young man I was sure must be our cousin stood in the entryway.

'Ah, Sam,' our uncle said, 'Glad I am that you're here to welcome your cousins, Enoch and Nathan.' He said our names gesturing to us each in turn.

Sam, who shared our family resemblance enough to be our brother, nodded a quiet greeting and turned into the house to make a path for us. He led us to a small but comfortable room under the eaves, saying little but seeming friendly enough.

Enoch and I unpacked our few belongings before rejoining our hosts in the family room. We were welcomed by a warm fire and cool ale, and our uncle offered us the most comfortable seats.

'So, you are here to learn more about being a successful Latin schoolteacher,' he announced. 'Yet, you attended Yale.'

I paused with my mug halfway to my mouth before noticing the twinkle in our uncle's eye. He began to laugh enthusiastically at his own joke and our unease. Enoch and I could only join him and therefore began to relax.

'Every one of my students has passed their college entrance exams,' Uncle Samuel said, puffing out his chest. When he did so, I was reminded that he was no weak scholar. His body retained some of the thick muscle from when he had served as a soldier in the war against the French and Indians.

'They dare not fail or face father's wrath,' our cousin added as he entered the room and took a chair near the fire.

Rather than take offense, the elder Samuel seemed to consider this possibility, eventually shrugging that there was likely some truth to this. I asked him how he balanced encouragement of his students with being a harsh taskmaster, but it seemed a skill difficult to explain to another.

'I would be happy to share my favorite classroom tools with you,' he said, deciding that this simpler task was more within my reach.

'That will be very helpful,' I agreed, and we planned to visit his schoolhouse the next day.

It had been a wearying day of travel, and our uncle was used to rising early. We, therefore, went to our beds.

Morning seemed to arrive seconds later, and I prepared to

join my uncle while attempting not to disturb Enoch. He could benefit from more rest since he had little need to visit the schoolhouse.

Joining my uncle and cousin in the kitchen, always the first room to be warmed in the morning, I was surprised to be handed a cup of tea. I tasted it, expecting a domestic herbal brew. The rich India tea was better than I remembered. We had grown adamant about refusing British imports at Yale, and I almost forgot that not everyone did the same.

'You do not participate in the boycott?' I asked without thinking that I might offend my host.

My cousin laughed while my uncle only shook his head as if in amusement.

'We do not,' Uncle Samuel admitted. 'I gave good years of my life fighting for the King, and I will not give up my tea as a token protest against him now.'

I took another sip, because I wasn't sure how to respond. And because it was delicious. Thankfully, my uncle continued, saving me from speaking.

'I was part of the last war and hope another does not come to plague our land. It was brutal and expensive. Anyone who experienced it knows how much it cost the British to protect their American colonies – our homes. I am happy to pay my taxes, just as I was willing to sacrifice myself for that cause.'

My cousin had a smug look on his face, as if he knew that I had not been too frequently exposed to this side of the story. I could almost hear him thinking that Yale men thought they knew everything but that was only because they didn't know how much they didn't know.

'You are at Harvard?' I asked him, changing the subject and approaching head-on what I thought was his complaint with me.

'Recently graduated as well,' he corrected. 'And studying law under my father.' He nodded toward the older man with obvious pride in claiming him. Whatever his faults, my cousin clearly loved his father.

'Perhaps we could write to each other,' I suggested, hoping to find more friendly ground. 'I, too, have considered taking up the law.'

Cousin Samuel only smiled thinly and tipped his head to me. My uncle gestured toward the door, so I took the opportunity to make my escape.

'I apologize for my son,' my uncle said once we were strolling along the road.

'Not necessary,' I assured him. 'He is proud of his father.'

A glimmer of a smile crossed his face, and I saw him consider whether he should say more before clamping his mouth shut and tipping his head to me in gratitude.

'Your first challenge will be growing accustomed to keeping students busy at every level so that none become idle and troublesome.' Thus begun, he went into a long lecture on demanding discipline in the classroom that did not end until we reached that destination.

'You have given me much to consider,' I said noncommittally as we entered the bright red structure.

Everything was neat and clean and in its proper place, and I was sure it did not only appear that way for the sake of my visit. Could I manage such perfection in my own schoolhouse? In my mind, I could see Enoch shaking his head at the suggestion. It made me smile, which my uncle took for appreciation of his domain.

'An organized schoolhouse is the first step toward a disciplined mind,' he recited, sounding like he had said it many times before. 'With God's blessings, many disciplined minds.'

I slowly walked around, touching desks and picking up slates. Would my schoolhouse be so well equipped? Wood was stacked near the hearth, and an empty pail stood ready to be filled from the well. I imagined a line of students waiting for their chance to dip their tin mugs in for a refreshingly cool drink.

'You will find it necessary to reward as well as reprimand,' my uncle continued. 'But if you keep their hands and minds busy, there will be less cause for trouble.'

'This I know, uncle,' I admitted with a grin. 'One of my dearest friends led me astray once or twice because he found his lessons too easy and his hands idle.'

'You see?' he said, vigorously nodding and pointing out some books and maps. 'You will need to develop methods for exciting the children's ambitions.'

I told him about our Linonia library and some of the titles I had contributed.

'Well done!' he exclaimed. 'It seems I have little to teach you, and I am forced to admit that Yale is producing fine young scholars.'

'Thank you, sir,' I said, dipping my head to him. 'I hope that I live up to your praise and expectations.'

We discussed some of his lessons and strategies for managing the classroom. By the time the sun was directly overhead, I was ravenous but he seemed content to continue his lecture until it had sunk below the horizon. Another hour passed before he glanced out the window and exclaimed that our dinner would be growing cold.

The schoolhouse was securely locked, and we strode quickly back to the house where we found Enoch and the younger Samuel waiting. They had retreated to opposite sides of the sitting room with their books. Although I knew Enoch enjoyed reading, it was not like him to do so when conversation could be made. I discerned that this was not our cousin's preference.

They rose and we went into the dining room, and I decided that I would try to break the ice between our cousin and us. Once we were seated, I smiled his way.

'Enoch and I enjoyed participating in the Linonia Society at Yale. It is a club for debate and rhetoric. Did you have something similar at Harvard?'

'A debate club?' he scoffed, belittling the beneficial hours we had spent discussing what I felt were important topics.

'More than that,' Enoch added. 'We discussed all sorts of questions, from mathematics to philosophy. It was quite enriching.'

Our cousin actually rolled his eyes, and I failed to understand why he disdained us so.

'It sounds like a useful endeavor,' Uncle Samuel said, giving his son a stern look.

'Nathan participated in a debate about the education of women at graduation and made quite a strong case for the fairer sex.'

I tipped my head to my brother but hoped he would stop supporting me quite so enthusiastically now. My cheeks felt warm, and I wondered what our uncle would think.

'Really?' he asked, in open curiosity, I thought, rather than the dismissal of so many of the older generation. 'I have taught only boys, of course. Do you have plans to invite girls into your classroom, Nathan?'

Enoch turned to me with his eyebrows raised. He had apparently not made this leap in logic.

'I have considered it,' I admitted, trying not to stare down at my food and avoid eye contact. 'I will establish my routine with the boys first but hope to be able to add some lessons for girls. What think you, uncle?'

Our cousin was looking eagerly at his father, as if he anticipated my humiliation a bit too keenly, but Uncle Samuel was nodding thoughtfully.

'I look forward to hearing the results of your experiment, nephew. Do write to me often from your post.'

I grinned, promised I would, and avoided looking at my fuming cousin.

Dinner continued with a few more half-hearted attempts to include Sam, but his attitude against Enoch and I was set in stone. We would leave soon, Enoch for home and I for my school, so there was little to be done but accept it.

When we left, our uncle was generous with food for our saddlebags and encouragement for our paths that would diverge from one another for the first time. We thanked him and promised to write before directing our eager mounts out of the city.

We rode in silence for some time. I didn't know what to say to my brother before parting, and he seemed to share my struggle. I felt as though I were planning to rend a limb from my body.

'You will write, Nathan?' Enoch finally murmured.

'Of course!'

He gave me a sidelong glance. 'It doesn't have to look pretty. Just write.'

I laughed and nodded. 'I will. And you must as well. And pray for me.'

It struck me that I would be leading my students in prayer rather than having my brother there to always say grace before meals or offer our thanksgiving before sleep.

When it was time for us to take separate ways, we halted our horses and dismounted before we spoke. Facing each other, we examined each other's features as if memorizing them. I had never needed to do this since Enoch was always at my side. I noticed details of his face I hadn't previously taken note of. He had a mole on his right cheek, and his eyebrows were too thin. Neither of us required shaving much yet, but wispy blond hairs on his upper lip reflected the sun.

I took a deep breath.

'How do we do this, brother?' I asked. My voice cracked.

Enoch grasped my shoulders. 'God goes with you, my dearest friend. You are going to be a blessing to your students. I have no doubt.'

I blinked rapidly, though Enoch allowed his tears to fall freely.

'Do not only write me sermons, preacher. I want news of the family.'

He nodded quickly and pulled me into a strong embrace. We stood that way long enough that the horses began stomping and snorting the need for us to be on our way, but I could not release him.

Finally, he patted me on the back and loosened his grip with a deep breath.

'We must each be on our way, Secundus.'

I nodded and smiled weakly. 'I must bow to the wisdom of my elder brother.'

With that, we climbed into our saddles and parted ways.

# Chapter 13
# Haddam Landing – December 1773

*There is existing in man, a mass of sense lying in a dormant state,*
*and which, unless something excites it to action, will descend with him, in*
*that condition, to the grave.* – Thomas Paine

I rode into the town of Haddam Landing and asked a man sweeping off the step of his shop to direct me to the schoolhouse. He looked up, squinting at me in a near-sighted way before deciding I appeared acceptable.

'You be wanting Moodus,' he said with a gesture vaguely directing me westward. 'Not far from the river.'

'Thank you, sir,' I said, directing my mount while hoping to find someone a bit more helpful as I continued on my way.

The town was nestled between large hills with some rocky cliffs hemming it in to the east and the Connecticut River to the west. It was a secluded kind of beauty, and I couldn't decide if it made me feel safe or trapped.

I came across a group of boys whose age I guessed to be about ten and hoped they might better direct me to the schoolhouse. They eyed me with some suspicion as I halted my horse next to them and looked down at them from my great height.

'Can you boys direct me to the schoolhouse?'

They looked at each other for a moment before one was brave enough to speak.

'Are you our new teacher?'

I decided to dismount. Standing not so high above them, I

admitted that I was. They looked from me to my horse and then to my bags. I was unsure what they hoped to find, but I seemed to pass their inspection. One pointed and the spokesperson, thankfully, added more detail.

'The schoolhouse is on a hill where the Salmon runs into the Connecticut.'

I assumed he was referring to rivers and nodded my thanks. 'Do you boys attend lessons?' I asked with a smile, hoping to sound encouraging rather than like a harsh taskmaster.

A few of them nodded. Some looked at the ground. Knowing it was not their fault if their parents could not afford school, I made an impetuous decision.

'Even if you don't, come by for some games in the evenings.'

They brightened at this, and I was assailed with several questions at once. I laughed and held up my hands to forestall their chatter.

'I did some wrestling in college, but I bet you lads like football.'

They grinned broadly and nodded enthusiastically.

'Very well,' I said, remounting my horse. 'I'll expect to see each of you. Thank you for the directions.'

They cried their farewells and waved as I rode toward the riverfront, and I felt I had made a decent enough start in what was to be my new home.

I found the schoolhouse quite easily at the junction of two rivers. The setting was pleasing to the eye, though the schoolhouse itself had been battered by wind, rain, and snow, leaving the red paint looking faded and distressed. Still, it looked sturdy - and it was mine.

The wind almost tore my hat from my head and carried the promise of snow, so I stabled my horse and went to inspect the schoolhouse. It had few windows, only two on each wall. That would keep it warmer in the winter, and river breezes would likely make them sufficient in the summer. A large hearth stood ready for a fire, but I did not see any wood. I pondered if I would need to chop some or if it would be delivered. Then I wondered what other details of my life here I had not considered before my arrival.

A knock behind me broke into my thoughts, and I turned to see a matronly lady holding out a dish covered by a towel. A delicious fragrance struck me at the same moment, and I closed my eyes to fully appreciate the sage, rosemary, and garlic.

'You must be Mr Hale,' she said, interrupting my thoughts already for the second time.

I laughed and stepped toward her. 'Yes, forgive me. I was hopelessly distracted by whatever wonderful meal you've brought.'

Her smile stretched across her face, and she blushed in a way that must have been becoming several decades ago. 'A young man must be well fed,' she stated as though it was she who was the teacher and held out the dish to me.

'Blessings to you. This is very kind,' I said, taking it eagerly, my stomach reminding me that it had been hours since I had stopped for a quick snack by the side of the road.

She patted my hand as the dish was exchanged and introduced herself. 'I am Hannah Pierson, and I live just across the way,' she gestured over her shoulder, leaving me no notion which house was actually hers. She carried on chatting away, referring to people I didn't know and places I had never seen. I smiled, nodded, and waited for a break in her speech.

'Why is it called Moodus?' I asked quickly before she could continue. Both the man and the children I had asked for directions had referred to Moodus when describing where the school was, and I'd no idea what they meant.

'Ha! That's what they call this part of town with its ghosts and rumblings is all.'

Before I could ask what she meant, she had changed subjects. It did not matter. I certainly wasn't afraid of ghosts or local legends and decided to think no more on it.

'Well, I shall not tarry,' she said after she had, in fact, tarried quite some time. 'I'll leave you to your dinner,' she nodded toward the cooling dish in my hands, 'and come by in the morning for the plate.'

'My thanks again, Mrs Pierson. God's blessings on your evening.'

I waited for the door to shut but no longer before I pulled the towel back from the plate steaming with roast beef, potatoes, and carrots. Dear Mrs Pierson could share her gossip with me as a daily habit if she provided such delicacies as this.


In the morning, boys began flowing through the door before the sun was in the sky. My eagerness matched theirs. I was, perhaps, a bit naïve about how smoothly the day would go and how many children would share my love of learning.

The initial settling was not a challenge, the pupils quieting almost instantly in their anticipation to see what their new schoolmaster would be like. Having been that young not long ago myself, I knew that they had been whispering about their expectations since they had heard of my upcoming arrival. Now, here I was to prove or disprove their rumors and guesswork.

I opened the day with a prayer that I then assigned to them for memorization. We would open each day with it going forward. I could already see which children rolled their eyes at this suggestion and which eagerly took to it. Some, already, I had failed to impress, and some others hoped to become my favorites. I observed them carefully, wondering which enjoyed being top students and which looked for my love to replace that which they did not receive at home. I smiled encouragingly at each one who noticed my gaze.

Then I moved to those who made no secret of not being about their assigned task. One little boy reminded me of Ben with his blond curls and thrust out chin that dared me to master him. I wondered if he also shared Ben's intellect.

'What is your name, young man?'

He mumbled so I could scarcely hear, 'Billy.'

'That's a good name. I have a brother named Billy,' I said, but he seemed unimpressed. 'Do you not wish to participate in morning prayer?' I asked him after I had leaned over closer to his eye level.

He glanced sideways at me, not willing even to turn his head in acknowledgement. Then he perfectly recited the prayer without glancing at the writing on his slate.

I felt myself grinning, though I knew this child would require discipline.

'That was very well done.'

He turned his head slightly my way but did not speak. I squatted down lower.

'Have you been bored with your schoolwork, Billy? Does it seem too simple?'

Now he gave me the gift of meeting my gaze full on. Billy searched my face as if wondering how I could possibly know. Then he nodded.

I stood and patted his shoulder. 'That is very good to know. I have a friend just like you. Not my brother,' I added with a wink. 'I'm sure I can find some topics to interest you.'

His eyes had followed my movements, and now his face lit

up. In a voice more sweet and submissive than that he had employed to recite his prayer, Billy murmured, 'Thank you, sir.'

I tried not to congratulate myself too heartily at my initial success as I visited other children who seemed tempted to nap or misbehave rather than set their minds to their memory work. After a few moments, we moved on to the next task, I foolishly believing that the morning had set the stage for the remainder of the day.

When we took our midday break, lunch pails rattled and cups were dipped into the water bucket at the front of the room. The quiet murmuring that accompanied the devouring of food soon rose to a cacophony of yelling and laughter that caused me to send them out of doors to run off some energy. I joined in a few of their games, trying not to give any one child more attention than the others.

They trudged back inside reluctantly, breathing heavily from their rambunctious play and flopping into their seats. It took some moments to calm them enough for our prayer of thanksgiving said after every meal, and then I instructed them to listen as I read from Rollin's *Roman History*.

Some listened intently while others clearly dozed. What I was not prepared for was those who refused to settle and began disrupting the reading. I ignored the low voices but could not continue when a piece of chalk flew through the air, resulting in giggles and angry exclamations.

'Everyone, take out your slates.'

The voices went silent, and slates clattered onto desks. I walked slowly around the room, but none of them met my eye, not even those who had been studious. I stopped before a boy who kept his hands in his lap.

'Have you no chalk with which to write?'

His wide eyes looked up to mine as he meekly brought up a

hand with a sliver of chalk caught between his fingers. I nodded and moved on. Hearing this exchange, others made sure their chalk was visible on their desk.

Except for one.

'Billy, where is your chalk,' I demanded. In my mind, I was seeing Ben throwing rocks at the windows of the dining hall. I resisted the urge to sigh.

Billy made a show of looking around his desk, on the floor, and in his pockets, before shrugging and giving me a convincing look of innocence.

This was God teaching me a lesson about the pain I had caused others, to be sure.

'Where is it?' I cast my gaze around the room, though I was uncertain any would admit to possessing the chalk.

To my surprise, a small boy timidly held it up. I walked over to him and put my hand out.

'It just landed by me, sir. I didn't...'

'I know you didn't. Thank you.'

I carried the chalk back to Billy and handed it to him. He seemed surprised. Returning to the front of the class and leaving Billy thinking he had gotten away with his misbehavior, I took up the book to continue the lesson before speaking again.

'Billy, please see that you fill the kindling box before you go home today.'

The way his face fell made me wish to retract my statement, but I knew how important it was to be kind but firm in the classroom. I continued the reading, trying to avoid Billy's eyes.

Not a minute had passed when one of the youngest boys screeched, making me jump and turning all eyes his way. His eyes were wide and glistening with tears when I rushed to his side.

'David put a spider on my desk!' he sobbed, pointing at a

grinning boy to his right.

Before I could even speak, a shriek came from the other side of the room, and I turned just in time to see an angry child yank on another's hair. Pandemonium ensued as if I had given the signal for it.

My unpreparedness overwhelmed me as I slowly turned, wondering which fire to put out first. A group of boys started running circles around the room, and I knew I had let things go too far.

'In your seats and cease talking, now!' I bellowed.

I admit that I was surprised when boys rushed back to their seats and some clamped hands over their mouths lest they be tempted to continue speaking. Staring them down, I was met by wide eyes and repentant countenances. I maintained my stern demeanor for the rest of the day, and it was exhausting just to keep peace in the room.

Once the other students were released that afternoon, Billy quietly filled the kindling box before murmuring an apology as he left. I was tempted to smile at his retreating form, but I was too weary. I rubbed my hands over my face and determined to get myself out of the schoolhouse as well.

I bundled up. The sun set early in these cold winter months. It felt good to stroll down the road along the river, despite the chill breeze that struck my face. It was refreshing and helped me clear my head of the chaos of the day.

Coming across a tavern, I decided to have a mug of ale and enjoy some conversation. The thought of it made me miss my friends, especially Enoch, and our Linonia meetings. I doubted the Haddam Landing pub would host discussions of Plato, but maybe I would find connections with others who shared my interests.

The smell of fish enveloped me as soon as I opened the

door, and I stepped inside to discover that this was a destination of dockworkers and fishermen. Their work had roughened their skin so that none seemed to share my youth though I was sure a few must. Distrustful glares were the closest I received to a welcome, but I persevered and approached the bar.

'New to town?' the tavernkeeper asked with a raised eyebrow. He looked up and down my inexpensive but well-tailored suit.

I cleared my throat and forced myself to smile. 'I am the new schoolmaster, Nathan Hale.'

He grunted in return and placed a mug of bitter ale in front of me before holding out his hand for a coin. I pressed my lips together into a thin line before handing it to him and turning around in the hopes of finding a friendlier face.

Discovering none, I slowly made my way around the room, sipping my ale, peering out windows, and nodding at strangers who did not invite me to share their table. I finished the mediocre brew and left, not a single soul having spoken to me.

It felt colder outside, but I was uncertain if the temperature had dropped or if my mood made it feel so. What I wouldn't give to have Ben or Isaac at my side. I walked for another mile or two but found no more welcoming tavern, so I returned to the schoolhouse and climbed to my loft.

My private space was fairly warm, benefitting from the fire kept burning in the schoolroom all day. I decided it was enough for me to forego a fire in the hearth and settled for a meal of cold meat, cheese, and bread before climbing under my covers.

Sleeping in a room by myself also felt odd, though it was not something a grown man could discuss with anyone. I had always shared a room with Enoch, and the last four years with Isaac and Elihu as well. Without their snoring and tossing, the room was disturbingly quiet, and I suddenly understood why so many unmarried folks had pets. My exhaustion overwhelmed these barriers to slumber, and I fell into a deep sleep.

I felt somewhat better in the morning, or at least convinced myself that I had to pretend as much as this was my lot in life. At least for now. I began to consider in greater depth what I wanted for a career. My Uncle Samuel may have made teaching his vocation, but I was more certain than ever that it was a temporary step for me.

Many of the children grinned happily at me as they stomped snow from their boots and entered the schoolhouse, and my spirits rose somewhat. Perhaps, I had been too discouraged by the single day. I took a deep breath and indicated that they should bow their heads for the morning prayer.

That was the last moment of quiet I enjoyed that day.

When my brother and I had gone for our lessons with Reverend Huntington, we had always been respectful and eager to learn. It was those lessons and our hard work that had earned us our places at Yale, and I suppose I had expected my own schoolroom to be filled with little Enochs and Nathans. I should have remembered that I had three older brothers who had chosen not to pursue collegiate studies.

After sending the children on their way that afternoon, I decided to walk in the opposite direction of the evening before. I hoped to find a more friendly tavern and needed to stretch my legs. Snow fell but the wind had calmed, so the streets seemed peaceful, especially compared to the chaos of the classroom.

Selecting a tavern with a welcoming façade and light glowing in its windows, I felt certain my time in Haddam Landing was about to improve. The ale was of a higher quality, and I was soon invited to sit with a group of men that seemed of an age with myself. I introduced myself as the schoolmaster, and they shared their names and vocations in turn.

'So, up in Moodus are you?' one asked, and I tilted my head at him.

'I've heard it called that before. Where does it come from?'

He repeated a story similar to that of Mrs Pierson about the neighborhood being haunted, and I decided it was best to let the subject go. I shrugged, mumbled something about that being interesting, and looked around the table hoping someone else would introduce another topic for discussion.

They made inane conversation about local goings on, so I decided to try again.

'What think you of the events in Boston?'

'You mean the dumping of the tea?' one asked in incredulity.

'Out of their minds, you ask me,' announced another before he gulped down half a tankard of ale.

'What of the monopoly on trade?' I inquired.

'The what?'

'It be a tax, that's what I heard.'

I took a breath and tried to explain, 'Parliament has given the East India Company sole rights to sell tea here in the colonies. It does not cost more, but it does not allow any competition in the market.'

They looked at me as if I had grown a second head and then shrugged at each other, taking up their mugs and their more comfortable conversation.

I sat back in my chair and quietly finished my ale as the realization hit me that I had little idea what life was like away from the company of learned men.

I spent a quiet, lonely Christmas in my loft above the classroom. At home, my sister, Eliza, was married to her Sam, but conditions made it impossible for me to travel for it. Besides an early winter storm raging through the region, I had not yet earned any wages, so all I had to my name was the horse father had gifted me and my Yale diploma.

It was with some chagrin that I posted my letter to the board of the New London school. Perhaps I hadn't given Haddam Landing enough time to become like a home to me, but no part of me wished for it to become so. Therefore, I was applying for the position of schoolmaster in New London, a city that I thought better suited to my taste. Whether I was too hasty, I cannot say, but the core of me screamed that I didn't have time to waste.

# Chapter 14
# New London – January 1774

*The bravest are surely those who have the clearest vision of what is before them, glory and danger alike, and yet notwithstanding, go out to meet it.* - Thucydides

The ride to New London with snow swirling down around me was the type of natural wonder Enoch would have enjoyed, though it left me chilled to the bone. It was no hardship for my mare who stomped and huffed as if it were great fun to prance through the fluffy stuff. I supposed that I had not given her enough exercise since I had begun my employment. Never had I anticipated the hours that I would spend preparing for lessons or arranging games for those who wandered back to the schoolyard for an evening more entertaining than one spent at home.

As soon as New London appeared on the horizon, I felt reassured in my actions. The port town was reminiscent of my beloved New Haven and did not share Haddam Landings' worn and weary appearance. The streets were bustling with people despite the cold, and I could see ships lining the docks in the distance. It already felt more like home than my windblown schoolhouse on the river.

I made my way to what I hoped would be my new schoolhouse. Its walls were painted a cheery red that stood out boldly against the falling snow. Four large windows on each side let in far more sunshine than my current schoolhouse would ever see. It was the shape of a small barn rather than the typical style, reminding me of Coventry and the family I dearly missed.

A man who I knew must be Timothy Green stepped out of the building and waved in my direction. He was the member of the Union School assembly with whom I was scheduled to interview. I smiled and waved in return as I dismounted and tied my horse to the hitching post.

'Hello, sir,' I said as I approached, trying to keep my voice from quaking with nervousness. Now that I had a better idea of how much I wanted this position, I was all the more afraid I wasn't prepared for this meeting. Yet, here I was.

'You must be Mr Hale,' he responded kindly with his hand held out to me.

I took it and felt myself relax a bit. 'I am, sir, and you must be Mr Green.'

He nodded in the affirmative and gestured toward the schoolhouse. 'Let us get out of the weather.'

I followed him into a pleasant classroom and glanced toward the loft, assuming that's where my rooms would be.

'If you are granted the position, one of our board members, John Richards, will provide you living quarters,' Mr Green corrected my thought, having noticed my gaze. 'You will have the upper floor for additional workspace to use as you see fit. I believe our current schoolmaster has something of a science lab above. Has the students experimenting with soils for growing different plants.'

'That's brilliant,' I said before stopping myself from praising the man I hoped to replace.

Mr Green nodded. 'He has done well here but has family obligations that require he leave in March.' He gestured toward a chair. 'Of course, that's why you are here.'

'Indeed.' I sat only after he had. 'I appreciate the opportunity.'

'I must explain that my recommendation will go to the board, but they have the final word on the position. However, I am greatly impressed by your recommendation from Reverend Huntington.'

I smiled and explained that Huntington had taught my brother and I since we were small boys and had prepared us well for our years at Yale.

'And how did you like Yale?' Mr Green asked, and I wished that I knew whether he was a Harvard man.

'Best years of my life so far.'

He laughed and looked back to the papers spread before him. He asked me about the Linonia Society and what I hoped to bring to the Union Grammar School.

'This will be different than your current position,' he pointed out while examining my countenance for reaction. 'As a Latin school, our pupils are preparing for collegiate work.'

'That is precisely what interests me, Mr Green. I wish to feed eager young minds the way Reverend Huntington did my own.'

I left out that my students at Haddam Landing had no such aspirations, but he must have guessed as much. We spoke pleasantly of the routine at Union and when I might reasonably hope to arrive if I were selected.

We had moved on to small talk, so I felt comfortable asking where the school got its name. Mr Green grinned as one does when invited to talk about what is impressive about their own hometown.

'A union of twenty gentlemen raised this school, painted it, and made it into what we hope is an ideal center for learning.' His arms spread wide to embrace the small structure as he explained.

He stood, so I did as well. We took a moment to appreciate

the fine new schoolhouse before he turned to me, his hand outstretched once again.

'I hope to be in touch with you soon, Mr Hale. I think you would do well here.'

I left New London eager to be called back permanently.

# Chapter 15
# Haddam Landing – February 1774

*Education is the kindling of a flame, not the filling of a vessel.* – Socrates

Back in Haddam Landing, I felt as though a dark cloud was hovering over me. It was easy to feel that way in the dark days of February, but it was more than the weather that bothered me. I tried as I might to love the students that God had sent my way in this gloomy little town, but my thoughts were more for those I imagined would greet me in New London.

I tried not to be overly eager about watching for a message from Mr Green and to keep my mind on the tasks at hand, but it grew increasingly difficult as snowdrifts and cold added to my feeling of isolation.

The wind shook my little schoolhouse as I stoked the fire, hoping to chase away a bit of the chill before children arrived for the day. Each student had a blanket draped over their chair, brought to school after the Christmas holidays in preparation for days such as this. The boys would be wrapped tightly in those covers today.

I placed the water bucket close to the hearth to melt the ice that had formed overnight. Most of the boys would bring a flask or jar of something warm to get them through the morning, but the water would be wanted in the afternoon. If it were still cold enough for ice inside the classroom at that point, I would have to dismiss them to their homes early anyhow.

As bundled up students began shuffling through the door, I soon realized that many would be missing. Haddam Landing boys found reasons to stay home throughout the year. It was too cold. It was too hot. It was time to help with harvest. I sighed at the lack of dedication.

'Can we sit around the fire, sir?'

I looked down to see Billy and smiled. He was one I would miss were I to leave this place, and I nodded my approval of his request given the few who had braved the snow that morning. Grabbing their blankets, the boys sat in a line with their backs warmed by the fire, and I pulled a chair over to sit before them.

We conducted morning prayers, reading, and some mental arithmetic in this way, but the room remained too cold for minds to be sharp or alert. I thanked them for being the brave few to show up and released them to make their ways home before another snowstorm made their way more treacherous.

A few days later, I had a letter from Mr Timothy Green inviting me to accept the position of schoolmaster at New London's Union Grammar School. I began penning my acceptance before finishing his letter.

# Chapter 16
# New London – March 1774

*I am very happily situated here. I love my employment, find many friends among strangers, have time for scientific study, and seem to fill the place assigned me with satisfaction.* – Nathan Hale

Thirty-two bright, eager faces looked toward me as I stood at the front of my new schoolhouse. My heart swelled. This is what I had hoped life would be for me in Haddam Landing, but it had not taken me long to find what I sought. This room full of open minds ready to learn was where I was meant to be.

As the days progressed, my satisfaction did not wane. I quickly realized that these boys were far ahead of the Haddam Landing boys in their curriculum and made appropriate adjustments, pleased to begin reading Greek mythology with them that had been far beyond the scope of my previous classroom.

Though the lessons were more challenging, the discipline was a much easier burden to bear, and I found myself turning over an idea that had been biding its time in the back of my mind. I decided to present it to my landlord, Mr Richards, to see if he felt it would meet the school board's approval.

The Richards house was pleasant, and I enjoyed having a room there rather than living above the classroom. The schoolhouse loft remained a science room as my predecessor had left it. It had pleased my employers and I could not immediately think of any better use. My living arrangements had another benefit that I could not have imagined during my interview.

Miss Elizabeth Adams had come to visit her aunt and uncle

Richards about the same time I had moved to New London. Therefore, we found ourselves under the same roof and sharing our explorations of the city.

A few years my junior, Betsey, as she had asked me to call her, was a vivacious girl with blond curls and blue eyes like something out of a romance novel. She held her own in conversation despite lacking the education I had enjoyed. Betsey listened attentively rather than dismissing topics the way other young ladies did. I was enraptured.

'Mr Hale, where has your mind wandered to?'

We were in the Richards' drawing room, and I smiled at Betsey as I gathered my thoughts back to myself.

'I was thinking of challenging the boys to a field day once the weather breaks.'

'It is important to exercise both mind and body,' she agreed gravely. 'What shall you have them do?'

My mind wandered back to my childhood on the farm and then to the grassy fields at Yale. 'Perhaps I should have them wrestle.'

Her eyebrows shot up, as I knew they would, and I laughed. 'Perhaps not.'

She shook her head at me and grinned. Some girls would feign offense at this sort of teasing, but not Betsey.

'I would not wish to have angry mothers bringing their sons' torn clothing to me, so I am thinking of foot races, an agility course, and ball throwing.'

Betsey considered these ideas, though I knew she had likely not participated in any such activities. I could imagine her holding up her voluminous skirts to try.

'It sounds like great fun,' she announced her judgement. 'I shall come to observe and serve snacks.'

'That is generous of you,' I said, casually tipping my head to her. My heart beat faster in my chest, and I couldn't help but wonder if she was simply looking to fill her time or wished particularly to spend her time with me.

She waved away my gratitude and stood, so I did as well. Her dress was homespun, but it did nothing to decrease her beauty. It cinched at her tiny waist, and I felt an almost overpowering urge to test if my hands could encircle it.

'I will say goodnight, Mr Hale.'

'Nathan, please.' I longed for her to use my Christian name.

'Nathan, then.'

She smiled up at me with the firelight making her glow like an angel. I gulped hard in order to murmur a goodnight.

The next day, I shared my plans for a field day with my boys and they cheered at the idea. A plea for warmer weather was added to our prayers, and I began making up a list of competitions.

It was not only for this reason that I keenly awaited spring flowers and summer sun. I was already envisioning Betsey on my arm as we walked along the waterfront. She would wear a large straw hat to keep the sun from ruining her creamy complexion, and I would thrill her with the story of Isaac and I surviving the storm in our little sailboat.

I had not been in New London for long, but my future was unfolding happily before my eyes.

# Chapter 17
# New London – May 1774

*Educating the mind without educating the heart is no education at all.* - Aristotle

Spring was in the air and my students were full of spirit, so I decided the day had arrived to take them outside for some physical activities. I directed them to set up some hogshead barrels in a line, and they attended to this duty with enthusiasm though they had not a notion for what they would be used.

That done, I gathered them around me for some announcements. 'We will have a series of races from here to the apple tree.'

I pointed and their eyes followed the gesture, their minds calculating how quickly they could cover the ground.

'We will also have ball tossing, starting there.'

I gestured to a spot not far off where throwers could face a recently plowed field. Some boys started swinging their arms to loosen up, preparing for this challenge. I grinned, knowing they would be shocked by my next challenge.

'And here,' I said, grasping the first in the row of barrels they had maneuvered into place, 'we will have a test of agility.'

They murmured excitedly and looked sideways at each other. The boldest of the group spoke up, 'What will we do?'

'I will demonstrate.'

I made a show of removing my jacket and rolling up my sleeves. Yanking my shirt untucked, I performed some stretches and then jumped a few times, pulling my knees up to my chest.

The boys were quiet and wide eyed as they waited in anticipation. I moved to stand before the line of barrels, looked at them, and winked.

When I leapt into the first barrel, I heard their gasps of astonishment. After I jumped from that one into the next, they began to cheer and grew louder with each leap. By the time I reached the end of the line of barrels, they crowded around me shouting uproariously and patting me on the back.

Then I saw Betsey standing behind them with a picnic basket over her arm. She blushed prettily when I caught her eye. I could only hope she had been impressed enough by my physical prowess to make up for my unkempt, perspiring appearance. I moved toward her, and the boys giggled and whispered as they took a step away.

'I thought you might select today for your field day.' She looked to the sky as she said this, letting the sun warm her face.

'You remembered.'

'Of course,' she said, squinting at me. 'I volunteered to help.' She lifted the basket, and I took it from her. It was heavily weighed down, and I wondered that she had carried it all the way to the schoolhouse. I placed it on a table the boys sometimes used to have meals out of doors.

'That is very kind of you, Miss Adams.'

She looked about to correct me, but then she became aware of the crowd of young boys gathered around us.

'My pleasure, Mr Hale,' she replied with a dainty curtsey that set them giggling again.

I turned to the boys and asked, 'Who thinks they can manage the barrel challenge?'

Betsey quickly forgotten, they cheered and raised their hands, eager to outperform their old teacher. I strove to form them into a somewhat organized line and watched Betsey move off to the side where she laid out the contents of her basket.

When Betsey and I strolled home that afternoon, we were both exhausted from keeping up with the students all day, but it was a contented feeling. I took her empty basket on one arm and offered her the other. She placed her hand in the crook of my elbow, and I felt that I had won the greatest competition of the day.

'What think you of the new acts passed by parliament?' she surprised me by asking when I was thinking of little else besides the warmth of her hand through my sleeve.

'I believe it will unify the colonies, rather than coerce them as is hoped. The men passing these laws know little of Americans.'

She nodded and waited for me to continue. Our footsteps slowed as if neither of us wished our walk to end too soon.

'They think by closing the port of Boston that other port cities will be afraid, and they are correct. Do you think the people of New London feel cowed into submission or angered into increased rebellion?'

Betsey took a moment to form her answer, as was her habit. She was not necessarily intimidated by my greater education, for she read the papers as regularly as I, but she did like to mull over multiple sides of issues before making a statement on them.

'I think you are correct. Do you believe those as far away as New York or even Charleston will feel the same?'

'That is difficult to say,' I admitted. I had never visited the Carolinas, so I could little imagine what the people there felt. However, I had to believe that some things were common to those of us in Britain's American colonies, regardless of the state to which we held allegiance. 'One can only wonder where this all will lead.'

'Not to war, I hope.'

She said it with a vehemence that surprised me.

'You do not wish for independence?'

Betsey sighed. 'I do not know,' she said, holding tighter to my arm and making me wonder why I cared about independence myself. 'I hate the idea of war more than anything. Fighting, illness, and death. All for what?'

'For liberty!' I exclaimed without thinking. What else could it be?

'But what does that mean?' she asked, stopping suddenly and turning to face me. 'Explain it to me, Nathan. I hear these lofty words, but what would be different? For you and me, right now?'

I gulped, not able to bring forth any brilliant argument for fighting when the most beautiful girl I knew was already here on my arm. What liberties had been denied me?

'It is not only about you and me,' I responded lamely, trying to remember the poor souls in Boston, out of work because of port closure and army occupation. It could happen here in New London.

Betsey frowned and turned to resume our slow stroll. 'Perhaps you are right, and I am being simple minded.'

'I would never call you simple.'

She rewarded me with a half-smile. It was a beautiful, sunny day, but she looked at me with clouds in her eyes.

'It scares me to think about it, Nathan. What will we endure and what men will die for these ideals?'

The back of my neck prickled as if chilled by a cold breath, but I had no answer for her.

# Chapter 18
# New London – June 1774

*If we mean to have heroes, statesmen, and philosophers, we should have learned women.* - Abigail Adams

'I have an idea.'

Betsey grinned and leaned forward.

'Tell me.'

We were sitting on a blanket near the waterfront on a fine summer day. My students were released to help on their family farms for the summer, which left me with time free for reading, letter writing, and courting my sweet Betsey.

'When the next school year begins, I would like to offer lessons to girls.'

I said this with some trepidation, not sure if Betsey would applaud the idea as an opportunity she herself wished she would have had or if she would be jealous of the time I spent in a classroom full of young women. I needn't have worried.

'What a wonderful idea!' she exclaimed, grabbing one of my hands in both of hers and giving it a heartfelt squeeze. 'I shall be the first to apply.'

Now it was my turn to be surprised. Why had I not considered the idea that Betsey would join my class? I laughed out loud. 'Are you making fun of me?'

Her smooth brow furrowed. 'How so? Do you not wish to have me as a student?'

I leaned forward and placed my hand on her velvety cheek. 'I can think of no one else I would rather be with - anytime, anywhere.'

She pulled away from me, blushing, but with a smile on her lips. 'You tease me,' she protested.

'Only if you enjoy being teased.'

Her blush deepened, and I was feeling emboldened. I lifted one of her hands and kissed it softly.

'Nathan...' she murmured but did not continue.

I knew not if this meant she wished for me to continue to press my suit or if I were embarrassing her here in this public venue, so I reluctantly released her hand.

'You can help me decide on a curriculum.'

She tilted her head. 'Curriculum?'

'For the girls' lessons?' I prompted with a grin.

'Ah, of course,' she laughed uncertainly at herself, which I found incredibly endearing. 'Some Shakespeare perhaps?'

'If it is your wish.'

'It is,' she asserted, having fully recovered herself and taken up my hand again.

Suddenly, I was happily anticipating the return to my classroom.

Too soon, it was time for us to stroll back to our lodgings. I made sure to keep our relationship strictly within bounds to ensure that I was not asked to find other rooms. Being under the same roof with Betsey was worth the effort, and the Richards seemed to encourage our courtship while trusting me to protect Betsey's reputation.

We arrived for supper, where the conversation grew intense. Betsey's Uncle John was livid regarding General Thomas Gage's arrival in Boston. I was concerned about what it all meant and wished Ben would visit with his stack of broadsheets as he had so many times during our Yale days.

'They say the fish caught in Boston Harbor still carry the flavor of tea,' Mr Richards stated. 'That will be the least of their troubles if these Coercive Acts are enacted.'

'I agree, sir,' I said, keeping my tone calmer and quieter than his. 'Parliament seems to have little idea or concern about how the people living in their colonies think or feel. Their legislation seems written with the goal of pushing us toward rebellion rather than increasing our willingness to submit to the crown.'

'Well said, schoolmaster,' he said, raising his glass. 'They are teaching you boys how to think up at Yale these days.'

That got a good-natured chuckle around the table, and I nodded as I raised my glass to his.

'Now, gentlemen,' Mrs Richards gently reprimanded. 'This is not appropriate for the table.'

'But why, auntie?' Betsey asked in an innocently curious voice. 'Should we not all be concerned and informed about the situation in Boston?'

Mrs Richards frowned. It was impossible to keep a proper table these days with talk of rebellion seeping into every corner of life.

'I apologize, my dear,' Mr Richards said before Betsey could press her case. 'You are right, as always. Mr Hale and I will have this talk over brandy once you ladies have taken your leave.'

Mrs Richards was assuaged by this. However, I was disappointed. I enjoyed my landlord's fine brandy but would have given it up to extend the conversation – any conversation – with Betsey present.

Oh, how Enoch and Ben would tease me if they knew.

# Chapter 19
# New London – September 1774

*The advancement and diffusion of knowledge is the only guardian of true liberty.* - James Madison

'The Suffolk Resolves.'

I held up a broadsheet covered in the tiniest print I had ever seen. Squeezed onto the page were the brave words of Bostonians who had met at a secret gathering of the Suffolk County Committee of Correspondence. If they could be brave enough to write it while surrounded by redcoats, I could at least share it with my boys.

'A copy of this was rushed by Paul Revere . . .' I had to pause as those who recognized the name boasted of what they knew. I cleared my throat after a moment to quiet them. 'He has taken a copy of these resolves to the intercolonial congress gathered in Philadelphia. Your task for this week is to read them and prepare to present your thoughts and discuss them.'

I held my hands up to hush them as I explained that they would all have a chance to read the broadsheet, which would be kept at an empty desk for each to take a turn. I indicated one to go first and instructed the rest to practice their arithmetic. After the sighs of those who must wait, they settled into their assigned tasks.

As I slowly made my way around the room, helping those with questions, I thought of the Suffolk Resolves and what they would mean for the future of the colonies. I was eager for the end of the week when my pupils would give their discourses. It would be like a Linonia meeting, and I knew they would share meaningful insights despite their youth.

'The Suffolk Resolves begin with a pledge of loyalty to George the Third,' a student named David began when each student had prepared their position. 'That is the last mention of our sovereign.' He looked at each of his classmates before carrying on, demonstrating his budding skill in rhetoric before continuing, 'This offense may make it difficult to seek peaceful negotiations with the crown. Yet, I believe that it was a purposeful snub meant only to give lip service to the king while detailing the Bostonians' intention to "defend and preserve those civil and religious rights and liberties for which many of our Fathers fought, bled, and died."'

David gave a little bow and took his seat as the next pupil stepped up for his turn.

'I agree with David,' he nodded to his classmate. 'And I was particularly interested in the resolve that "altering the established form of government" in the colony of Massachusetts was a "gross infraction of these rights to which we are justly entitled by the laws of nature, the British constitution, and the charter of the province."' He turned toward me. 'It caused me to wonder if parliament and the king have the right to alter the Massachusetts government since it is they who gave the powers to the colonial assembly.'

'Very good,' I said. 'I am pleased to hear each of you thinking beyond the words of the resolves to consider whether you agree with them. What do the rest of you think of William's point?'

I allowed the free flow of conversation for a few moments before holding up a hand.

'These are the very same issues being discussed in

Philadelphia,' I reminded them, and I saw a few of them puff out their chests a little bit. 'It is important that you are informed citizens in addition to being kind and generous Christians.' They nodded gravely in agreement, making me smile. 'Very good. Continue.' I gestured toward the next student.

'I have a question as well,' he began. 'When the resolves speak of "the attempts of a wicked administration to enslave America," are they making a distinction between parliament and the king? Also - two questions I suppose. Does this distinction matter? Will not the king be offended either way?'

I grinned, both because I was indeed pleased, and I wished him to know that I thought no less of his decision to pose an inquiry rather than state his thoughts. After the class had discussed these issues for a few moments, I had him come closer.

'It is a strong sign of a critically thinking mind to inquire regarding the thoughts of others rather than simply imposing your own beliefs. Well, done.'

He happily returned to his seat, and the students continued their discussion of the Suffolk Resolves until it was time to break for our meal and some time out of doors. I was encouraged to see several students demonstrate an aptitude for rhetoric and debate that would serve them well as they journeyed forth to the university of their choice.

Word had spread around town that I was to begin a girls' class, but I pulled at my collar and reorganized my desk for the third time that morning as I waited to see if any would take up my offer. When the door creaked open, I turned to see Betsey standing there with the sunrise palette glowing behind her.

My breath caught in my throat at the heavenly vision she was, and it took me a moment to realize that others were striding in behind her. Most were younger than Betsey, and I felt my jaw drop as they kept flowing in her wake. Once they had taken seats, I scanned the room for a quick count.

Twenty young ladies sat at the desks, gazing up at me with eager eyes. I closed my mouth and smoothed the front of my jacket, taking a moment to compose myself. I had expected six, maybe ten. But Betsey had brought twenty. Bless her.

'We will start out with morning prayer,' I began, just as I did with the boys on each first day of term. They were attentive to this task and just as quick to memorize and recite. Some of them glowed with satisfaction at their accomplishment, and it made me wish I had more than the two hours before the boys arrived to devote to them.

Seven of the clock arrived sooner than I could have imagined, and the ladies took their leave to attend to their chores and duties for the day as the boys began arriving. Betsey blew me a kiss on her way out the door that served to warm me for the remainder of the day.

'Nathan, have a drink with me!'

I was leaving the schoolhouse for the day and found Stephen waiting for me in the street. I had recently discovered that he resided in New London. Though we had not been close friends at Yale, it was a bond that brought us together now. Betsey understood how much I missed the companionship of Ben and Enoch and was not jealous of my time with Stephen, but instead was happy that we were well suited.

'Gladly,' I agreed, trotting to catch him up.

We strolled along companionably. I told him how well my students were progressing, and he shared some of his past escapades set within the tavern to which he directed me. We were laughing by the time we entered the ramshackle place and thirstily ordered mugs of ale.

'So, I hear you've begun instructing the ladies,' Stephen said suggestively.

I rolled my eyes and gave him a gentle shove. 'You should know, they are quite studious.'

He laughed loud enough that a few patrons looked our way. After a moment, he glanced at me and brought himself under control. 'You're serious?'

'Entirely.'

'And they come at dawn?'

'Five of the clock,' I clarified.

Stephen shook his head in wonder. 'If I could compel young ladies to do my will, I would use that power for something besides getting them to lessons too early in the morning.'

I ignored his implication and defended my students again. 'That is the only time I have available for them, and they are eager to learn.'

He stopped shaking his head only long enough to take a long pull from his mug. We sat in affable silence for some moments, relaxing and enjoying the ale, which was attentively refilled.

Another man strolled up to us and slapped Stephen firmly on the back. He jumped to his feet to embrace the newcomer before turning back to me.

'Nathan, let me introduce Gilbert Saltonstall.'

I shook his hand and gestured toward an empty seat. 'Do join us, Mr Saltonstall.'

'Please, call me Gil,' he said, taking the proffered seat and waving to the tavern maid for a drink.

'You two have perhaps seen each other before but don't

remember,' Stephen said as Gil's mug was placed before him. 'Gil graduated from Yale in 1770.'

'Ah, wonderful,' I said. 'I am class of 1773.'

We clinked our mugs together and drank deeply.

'Exercises will start next week,' Gil said to Stephen.

'Militia,' Stephen said to me in explanation. 'Our regiment is out of practice and who knows if we may be called upon.'

I nodded and drank again to avoid having to speak. Gil and Stephen talked about when and where drills would be performed.

'We will have our own liberty pole before we know it,' Stephen declared, slamming his mug down to emphasize his point.

'I must wonder how this will impact my father's business,' Gil said, more contemplative than Stephen in these matters.

'What is his business,' I inquired.

'Mercantile. It is where I am currently employed. The Boston port closure has had its impact, and I fear things will only get worse.'

I frowned and nodded, not sure I had an encouraging word to share.

'And what do you do?' Gil asked. I saw Stephen smiling behind his mug, clearly thinking of my female students again.

'I am the schoolmaster at Union Latin School.'

'Ah, I've heard good things about it,' Gil said.

'Thank you. I enjoy my employment. It gives me fulfillment, if not the companionship of my Yale days. I find I often learn from my students even as they learn from me.'

'As it should be. You must be a good teacher.'

I tipped my head in thanks and took up my mug.

'You should join us, Nathan,' Stephen insisted, and I raised an eyebrow at him. 'At the drills. Join the artillery company.'

My brain went a bit fuzzy at the suggestion, more so than

from the ale. Talk of war preparations had been going on for years, so I could not explain my shock at this invitation. I stuttered, 'I shall consider it,' and would commit no further.

When we left the tavern, it had grown dark. The sky was clear of clouds, leaving the stars free reign to sparkle brightly. Before I realized where we were going, we arrived at a large meadow, and I wondered if Stephen had directed us here to cajole me into artillery practice.

'Schoolmaster, what constellations can we see at this time of year?'

I gazed up at the sky and could hear Enoch's voice in my head. *Isn't it beautiful, Nathan? Only God could create such a wonder.*

Gil flopped down on the ground, and Stephen and I followed suit. Looking up at the swirls of distant galaxies made one feel quite insignificant.

'Cygnus,' I said, pointing toward the north.

'The Swan.'

I glanced over to see Stephen sigh contentedly. He may perform military maneuvers because it was his duty, but he studied the heavens because it was his passion.

'Delphinus,' he said, pointing, but I had no way of discerning which of the thousands of stars he meant. 'It is like a bright diamond,' he added, realizing that neither Gil nor I knew the constellation. After a few moments of gesturing and correcting, I was fairly sure I had found it.

We had been there long enough that the ground grew cold beneath me, and I stood stiffly.

'I must get to my bed,' I said with regret. 'I must rise early.'

'For your ladies,' Stephen couldn't resist one last jab.

I took it in stride, bowing my head in admission. 'It is a fine class of scholars.'

'Oh, if you must,' Stephen said. He and Gil also rose.

We walked home, saying our farewells as each had to turn down a street toward our own lodging. It was the first time since leaving Yale that I felt the comradery of friends, and I was warmed by it despite the cold specter of war.

# Chapter 20
# Coventry – December 1774

*If we love one another, God dwelleth in us, and his love is perfected in us.* - 1 John 4:12

Content as I was in New London, I was eager to visit my family for the Christmas season. My mare was glad to be free of her stable as well. I did not ride her often enough during the school term, so she pranced happily as we covered the thirty miles to Coventry.

My mount seeming to know her way, I allowed my mind to wander back to the moments I had shared with Betsey before leaving. I had acquired a book of poems by Alexander Pope and wrapped it in linen. When I presented this gift to her, complete with red ribbon, she surprised me by offering me a gift in return.

'Dear Betsey,' I had started before she halted my words with a finger to my lips.

'Do not say I should not have bought a gift for you. I wanted to.'

'Very well. I will treasure it.'

She laughed. 'You do not know what it is yet.'

'It matters not. It is from you.'

She blushed and tried not to smile.

'Open it,' she ordered.

The silver shoe buckles she had presented to me were carefully packed in my saddlebags. I would not risk losing one as I traveled.

She had squealed when she opened the book and

immediately tied the ribbon in her hair. I would swear I could still feel the warmth of her kiss upon my cheek.

I arrived at my childhood home feeling something like a stranger. This time, I had not even my brother at my side, and it felt odd for him to greet me as a visitor, as happy as I was to see him.

'Enoch, I have much to tell you,' I said, embracing him firmly and releasing him with reluctance.

'Praise God for your safe arrival,' he said as he scanned my face for signs of distress as though he were my mother.

'I am well,' I assured him. 'How go your studies?'

'Quite well, I believe. I hope to take my licensing exam within the year.'

'That's wonderful.' I slapped him on the back. 'Not that I am surprised. You were born to be a preacher.'

'God has a plan for us all,' he agreed. 'And how is His plan working out for you, brother?'

I was retrieving my bags so that my younger brother, David, could see to my horse. Turning back to Enoch, I said, 'I love my employment. I have thirty-two boys and twenty scholars of the fair sex. Having found a few friends among the strangers, I am quite content.'

'Many blessings.'

'Yes.' And I had not even told him about Betsey yet. That would be saved for later, when we could share some private moments over a bottle of wine. 'And now I am here with you. I could ask for nothing more.'

'Amen,' he said with a grin.

With that, Enoch backed away to give our brothers and father their chance to properly greet me. I missed Eliza, who now had her own homestead, but I would see her soon.

My chest tightened when my father had his turn to approach me. He looked older than he had a few months ago, and he seemed to lean upon his wife for support. For the first time I wondered how much time we would have with him here on earth. He was not old, but neither was he young, and the times were uncertain.

'My schoolmaster,' he said by way of greeting with his eyes full of pride. He took his arm from around my stepmother to firmly grip my arms. 'You are working hard?'

'Of course, father. Is there any other way?'

He nodded, satisfied. 'Come inside. Your sister has baked cakes for you. And my goodwife has brewed a pleasing cider.'

I was confused for a moment before I realized he meant my younger sister, Joanna. I tried to calculate her age as I followed father inside. I remembered her as a small child but standing there in the kitchen was a young woman of twelve. She looked so much like our mother that tears sprung to my eyes, and I surreptitiously wiped them away.

'Nathan,' she squealed, now sounding more like the child I remembered. Joanna threw herself into my arms and I swung her around, hoping she was not too old for such play. She beamed at me with her cheeks flushed when I placed her on the ground.

'You shall not be able to stay long,' she announced with mock sternness. 'If the girls in the village are reminded what a handsome brother I have, I shall be plagued with false friends.'

My brothers erupted with objections that she already had them, but she remained silent and only winked at me. I looked forward to getting to know her better, though I had known her since the day she was born.

Supper was a raucous affair, with my siblings vying for my

attention as if I weren't going to be visiting for a fortnight. Only once the rest had gone off to their beds did Enoch and I have time to ourselves before the hearth.

'This is a fine vintage you've brought,' Enoch said as he sipped the red wine I had acquired through Gil. I told my brother about this new friend.

'You have also met a lady,' Enoch said once we had agreed that neither of us remembered Gil from Yale.

I arched an eyebrow his way. 'Does God speak to you now that you are to preach His word?' I joked as I topped up our glasses.

Enoch chuckled. 'No more than He speaks to us all, but I am your brother – your friend. I can tell.'

In front of anyone else, I would have felt the heat of embarrassment, but it was comforting that Enoch and I retained our connection though we were no longer together day-by-day.

'Her name is Betsey.'

I suddenly realized that I did not know where to begin.

'She must be an exceptional young lady, for I know none other who has left my brother tongue-tied.'

I had to laugh at myself, and then I told him about the woman who had stolen my heart.

We stayed up late into the night, catching each other up on our lives and plans. We did not speak of the portent of war, but its presence was felt in the room like a restless ghost.


The next day, Joanna was once again busy in the kitchen when I came downstairs in need of a hot mug of tea. Expecting a homemade herbal blend, I was surprised by the rich, black cup set before me. When I raised questioning eyes to my sister, she hushed me with a gesture. Surely, this was some secret stash leftover from before the boycott. I relished it, breathing deeply of its aroma before sipping it slowly.

Joanna chatted about her friends in the village, most of whom I remembered as children if I remembered them at all.

'Perhaps I should play the matchmaker,' she teased, peering at me with a critical eye.

'No need for that, dear sister. The only women I hope to entertain while I'm home are you and sweet Eliza. When shall we see her?'

Joanna took pity on me and shared news of Eliza and her Sam. She shocked me by adding, 'They've no baby on the way yet, much to Eliza's dismay.'

I wasn't sure how to respond to this women's business, so I raised my empty mug and pretended to drink. Joanna shook her head at me and held out the teapot to refill my cup.

My brothers started filing in to save me from further discussion of Eliza's hopes to conceive. David reassured me that he was heading straight out to the barn to care for my horse, while Billy and Richard attempted to talk over each other about joining the war effort as if they need convince me which was the greater patriot. Father and his wife entered the kitchen at that moment, immediately putting an end to the chaos.

Although my brother was almost a reverend in his own right, it was my father who blessed the table before we tucked in to the bounteous meal to break our fast. It made me realize how much I appreciated my simple but independent life in New London.

Joanna had not yet cleared the table when a voice called from the front door.

'Where is that brother of mine?'

And though Eliza had eight brothers, all eyes were on me. I jumped from my seat and was to her in the blink of an eye. Once

I had squeezed Eliza too firmly and she had smacked me to release her, I held her at arm's length just to look at her.

'You are as beautiful as ever,' I said and meant it. Her golden curls escaped her cap as they had ever since she was a child, and her blue eyes danced with happiness.

She swatted me again and demanded to know who had been feeding me. A few more questions about my living conditions and schoolhouse apparently satisfied her, and she moved on to greeting the rest of our siblings.

They, of course, were not as excited to see her since they lived in the same village all the time. I, on the other hand, was pleased to sit and listen to her talk about Sam's medical practice and hear the pride in her voice when she mentioned her own little house.

'Sam is working now?' I asked.

'Always,' she said with a small sigh. 'Illnesses and accidents come on their own schedule with no respect for holidays and visitors.'

I laughed and took her hand, 'I will get to know him later. This way I have you all to myself.'

'And me!' objected Joanna as she joined us at the table having finished her morning duties.

They spoke a bit about women's things, and I was content to simply be in their company. It was a wonder to me that these were the same girls I remembered, and I considered whether the changes in myself were as drastic to them.

My time in Coventry was over so quickly that I found myself recounting the days to ensure I had correctly calculated. I was sad to say goodbye to my family, but the thought of seeing Betsey again urged me forward. Perhaps, when I next visited, she would be at my side. The idea thrilled me and gave me the strength to say farewell to Enoch once again.

After he had admonished me for failing to write often enough, we became more serious.

'You will tell me if you join the militia,' he commanded. Perhaps he had become surer of himself without me constantly at his side.

'I will,' I agreed, still uncertain about whether my place remained solely in my classroom, but Enoch had already discussed this at length.

'And you will send me a copy of your first sermon as a licensed reverend.'

He grinned and pulled me into an embrace. I wanted to tell him that I missed him at my side, that life was so different on my own, but I had to be satisfied that he knew.

'Godspeed, my brother,' he said, and I was off.

# Chapter 21
# New London – March 1775

*Is life so dear, or peace so sweet, as to be purchased at the price of chains and slavery? Forbid it, Almighty God! I know not what course others may take; but as for me, give me liberty or give me death!* – Patrick Henry

I folded the letter in my hand and sat back contemplating its contents. Some of my friends who remained at Yale wrote of drilling on campus. The school was thick with patriotic fever and demonstrated it by preparing to serve.

The words convicted me of my own failure to act. Gil and Stephen had invited me to join the artillery drills in New London months ago, but I continued to fail to find time to join them.

I wished, not for the first time, that I could discuss these issues with Ben. We wrote to each other, but it was not the same thing as hashing issues out over books and broadsheets as we used to. He had not yet joined his local militia either, and I wondered if we were not both similarly trapped between our desired future and our ideals.

Unfolding the letter again, my eyes were drawn to one phrase.

*We see great evidence that war will be proclaimed soon.*

Was it true? Or was it the boasting of a college boy wishing to prove himself a man through the bloodshed of war?

I understood part of this desire. The time I had passed with Betsey made me wish to marry her, but I dared not consider the thought while my living was scarcely sufficient to keep me in rented rooms. Could military service raise me up to a higher position that would enable me to make my proposal?

A walk would clear my head, so I pulled on my cloak and hat before stepping out into the brisk day. The wind was ever swirling through the streets as it did in most waterfront towns, so I pulled my scarf up to partially cover my face. I breathed in the chill air as deeply as I could with this barrier in place. Walking down the deeply rutted street, I asked God for a sign.

'Make the path before me clear,' I asked in a low voice that none other than my Lord could hear through the scarf and wind.

At the port, I saw cannons being moved into position. They pointed out over the bay, and I wondered if they would ever have cause to fire at a British ship. Although words of discontent and possibility of war had been spoken for as long as I could remember, the physical proof that fighting might come right here to New London sent shivers up my spine.

Convinced that I could no longer wait to see what would happen like a spinster sitting in the corner at a village fete, I strode purposefully toward Stephen's lodging.

'If it remains extended, I would like to accept your invitation,' I stated as soon as he opened the door to my knock.

He grinned, needing no explanation of what I spoke.

'Richards will assist you with the required uniform.'

I nodded, accepting this charity since the white broadcloth coat and breeches were not within my budget.

'Gil should be able to procure a musket,' Stephen continued, and I only nodded again.

'We have always governed ourselves. We always mean to. They don't mean that we should.'

I needed no further convincing, but I stood up straighter and agreed, 'The British shall not rule us as second-class citizens.'

He grasped me by the shoulder. 'Not when we have honorable men willing to fight for liberty.'

I was not ready to proclaim yet, as Patrick Henry had, 'Give me liberty or give me death,' but I had taken a step closer.

'We have been waiting for you, Nathan. Welcome to the New London Artillery Company.'

# Chapter 22
# New London – April 1775

*When liberty is the prize, who would shun the warfare? Who would stoop to waste a coward thought on life? We esteem no sacrifice too great, no conflict too severe, to redeem our inestimable rights and privileges.* – Dr Joseph Warren

I soon discovered that artillery drills were not as thrilling as young boys believe. When we play at war as children, there is constant action and the great benefit that nobody dies. Moving through the drills was tedious, but I took great satisfaction in our improvement and ability to work well together. It was these unexciting details that could save lives.

My attention was drawn to a boy running across the meadow to where we worked. I recognized him from my classroom, so I moved to meet him. He almost stumbled into me, his breath coming in gasps as he struggled to impart his message.

'Shots . . . . fired . . . . Concord . . .'

'Just breathe,' I urged him. I patted him gently on the back as if everything inside me wasn't screaming to know his full message.

'And Lexington,' he finally managed as he gulped in the warm spring air. 'They are just north and west of Boston, sir.'

His breath was coming normally now, and it was mine that I was sure had stopped.

'Battle? Not like the riot - the Boston Massacre,' I clarified for the boy would only know it as such.

He nodded quickly. 'Engagement of the enemy,' he assured

me, and I fleetingly wondered where he had heard that phrase.

'Casualties?'

'On both sides, sir. The British have retreated to Boston.'

I looked back at my company as they played at war and wondered how long we had until real ammunition flew through the air around us.

News poured in from other towns in the coming days. The British had attempted to secure weapons, not to mention the persons of Samuel Adams and John Hancock, but they had failed on all counts. I wondered what other patriots had been forced to leave Boston now that fighting had begun in earnest – and where the next shots would be fired. Both sides would be emboldened by the losses they had suffered.

A town meeting was called to discuss New London's response to the battles at Lexington and Concord. The British were besieged in Boston, and some believed we should take the fight directly to them. Would it send them scurrying across the ocean or bring down the awful wrath of the greatest military in the world?

Of course, there were also those who wished to wait for more news or a response from London or whatever that *something* was that would spur them into action. I had read enough history to know that timidly waiting for the right moment rarely led to victory. Though I was young and not native to New London, I stood.

'Let us join our brothers in arms in their stand against tyranny. I will go. Who is with me?'

I was surprised how many men loudly roared their agreement once one had stood to boldly speak. I had to yell to be heard over them.

'Let us march at once and never lay down our arms until

independence is won!'

I could scarcely believe myself, but I felt infused with the strength of my friends and loved ones. It was for their liberty and peace that I was willing to fight.

I tried to hold on to that passion the next day when I had to tell my pupils that I would be leaving. Many of the boys clearly wished they could go with me, and I had to pray that it would not come to that even as I reassured them that they would get their chance.

I answered their questions, such as I could, about the siege of Boston and the plans of the patriots. I knew not when a new schoolmaster would arrive or who it would be, but I could not wait.

'Why must you go?' one boy, not romanced by the idea of war, timidly asked.

I held up my hand to stave off those who would call him a coward or a Tory.

'A man must follow the path the Lord sets before him and ought never to lose a moment's time once he discerns it. If he put off a thing for one minute to the next, his reluctance is but increased.'

My student appeared content if not entirely convinced by this wisdom, but I knew that I could not veer from the road I had been set upon.

'We must do one more thing together before I leave,' I said, and the boys quieted themselves and bowed their heads with no further instruction. We prayed for the safety of those we loved, especially those tasked with protecting our liberties. As always, we begged God for guidance and strength, and then I closed the final prayer I was to share with my New London boys.

# Chapter 23
# New London – June 1775

*Love and Duty where, and in Proportion as, it is due.* – John
Adams

Betsey's small, soft hand was in mine as we gazed out over
the dark water. The sight would normally give me an unsettled
feeling. I didn't like the thought that so much life and death
swirled under the waves just outside our view. But with Betsey at
my side, the scene was as beautiful as she was, though she was
golden and light in contrast to the dark of the evening sky and
harbor waters.

I turned to her, my feelings a kettle of confusion bubbling
inside of me. I longed to kiss her, to touch her, but that urge could
not compare to my need to protect and shelter her. My desire
would not be the cause of her damaged reputation, so I contented
myself with stroking the impossibly soft skin on the underside of
her wrist.

She smiled up at me, and I wondered if she, too, was
struggling to sort her feelings for me. I thought of that first dawn-
break I had seen her step into my classroom, eager to learn and
certain there was a new world ready to greet her.

I had tried to think of her only as a student.

'What are you thinking?' she asked, and I laughed aloud,
for where could I begin.

She was not discouraged. 'I was thinking of A *Midsummer
Night's Dream*. You set my heart aflame when we read it in your
little schoolhouse.' She locked her eyes on mine. 'Did you know?'

I took a deep breath, shocked by her forwardness. Then I considered her question, which was difficult to do when she was looking at me this way, here and now.

'I must confess, I don't know that I did.' I shook my head ruefully, and she laughed in forgiveness. 'We men can be a bit slow-minded when it comes to matters of the heart.'

She moved closer, facing me, and I felt my body respond to her nearness, her citrusy floral scent.

'Then I will help you,' she stated, as if she did not share my physical turmoil. She dropped my hand and grasped my arms, and I felt my biceps flex in response to her touch. She smiled.

'Do you love me, Nathan Hale?'

I pled with my heart to regulate its beating. This was the most important question I had ever answered, and Linonia debates had not sufficiently prepared me. She tilted her head. I was taking too long.

'I do.' I cleared my throat. 'I love you, Betsey Adams.'

She beamed, and I couldn't help grinning in return.

'And I love you,' she whispered. Then she shocked me again by asking, 'Just what are we going to do about that?'

I kissed her. I hadn't thought about it. Could hardly believe I was doing it. And then I realized she wasn't submissively accepting of my affection. She was returning it. Her soft lips caressing mine in a slow languid way that promised more.

But not now.

She gently pulled away and examined me. I raised my eyebrows, having no idea what I must do or say to pass her inspection.

'I have a mind to marry you, Nathan.' Her hands moved up and down my arms but no further. I had the sudden desire for her hands to reach my skin, to travel further. Did she realize how difficult she made my concentration?

'But.'

She retrieved my focus.

'I will not marry a militia man.' She released my arms, and I felt their absence in the cool breeze upon my body no longer warmed by her touch. I tried to clear my head without literally shaking it.

'I do wish to marry you, Betsey, but I do not believe your uncle would give his permission. My salary...'

'He would,' she cut my objections short, and I was already imagining her, dressed in sunny yellow, standing before the preacher, joining me in our bridal bed. 'But.'

That rude interruption again.

'I will not marry a militia man,' she repeated. 'I have watched too many women struggle alone, too many grieve a man who never returned from the last awful war.' She paused and looked out over the harbor, and I wished I could read her mind the way I could the pages of a book. Then she turned. 'That war lasted seven years. I will not sacrifice so many years to a husband who is not at my side.'

My mind was a jumble. I wanted her more than anything. But I also deeply felt my duty to my country. What man stayed home when that home required defending?

'I know you need time to think about this,' Betsey said, placing her hand on my cheek. I closed my eyes and leaned into it, imprinting the sensation in my mind.

I opened my mouth, but she placed a finger on my lips.

'Do not attempt to answer me now. I would rather have your thoughtful, considered response than your impetuous reflex that you might later regret.'

Betsey slowly lowered her finger and backed slightly away. I considered taking her into my arms, kissing her again, and promising to marry her as soon as banns could be posted. She seemed to be watching these thoughts course through my mind and waiting to see if I would act upon them. She tilted her head at me again, and then turned and walked away.

I looked out to sea and wondered if I had just made the biggest mistake of my life.

# Chapter 24
# New London – July 1775

*Our holy religion, the honor of our God, a glorious country, and a happy constitution is what we have to defend.* – Benjamin Tallmadge

My time was fully consumed with training troops and preparing the defenses of New London. During quiet moments before I fell into exhausted sleep, I sometimes thought of my schoolhouse and the students that filled it. Always, invading the corners of my mind was Betsey.

She did not treat me coldly, but neither did we share intimate moments or even strolls through town. The polite but distant relationship caused scorching pains in my chest, but I could not give her the promise she demanded. I could not fathom watching on as an observer when the time came for us to join the troops at Boston, even if I would do so with Betsey at my side.

A recent letter from Ben had hardened my resolve, and I knew that I must sacrifice my present happiness with Betsey for the promise of something greater in the future. Ben insisted that it was time we both do our duty to our God and our country. He was right, of course, as Ben always was. I could only pray that Betsey would eventually see it that way . . . and that she would wait for me.

That evening over supper, Mr Richards held up his glass and the rest of us followed suit.

'Congratulations to Mr Hale are in order,' he began, and I saw Betsey's features cloud over. 'I heard you have been named sergeant.'

Murmurs of congratulations came from around the table as our glasses clinked together and I bowed my head to each in thanks.

When my eyes met Betsey's, she quickly looked away. I considered standing up and proposing to her right that moment, but I would neither force her to accept me under duress nor embarrass us both with a public refusal.

I accepted the kind words of the others before making my excuses and retiring early. Thankfully, the physical labor of the day enabled me to quickly fall asleep despite the confusion of my mind and conflict in my heart.


The next day I wrote to Enoch and poured out my heart as much as a man could. Meaning I announced my commissioning as sergeant and admitted that Betsey was fearful of what duty the position entailed. It was as close as I came to confessing the ultimatum she had presented.

Had I really rejected her? I felt that I was the one set aside, but as I replayed the events in my mind, I was horrified at my actions and determined to speak to her again.

I posted the letter to Enoch, hoping that I would have happier tidings to send him in my next missive. Then I went to find Betsey.

She was in the Richards' drawing room, so engrossed in a book that she did not notice my approach. When I cleared my throat, she jumped a little, but her face cleared into a happy smile when she looked up at me.

My heart almost burst. I could mend what I had broken. Her eager, loving face told me so.

I moved forward quickly, kneeling before her. A blush

flamed across her face, but she eagerly met my eye.

'Betsey,' I said, sounding like I was pleading, but I suppose I was. I took her hand. 'I cannot tolerate the coldness between us. Can you ever forgive me for being an unthinking dolt? I do love you and should never have allowed you to doubt it for a moment.'

Tears shone in her eyes, but her smile was ecstatic. I pressed my case.

'Betsey, marry me. God has placed us here together for a purpose. Do you feel the same?'

'Oh, Nathan,' she said in a breathless whisper. 'You know I love you. Of course, I will marry you.'

I felt as if I could fly, and I took her into my arms. She kissed me boldly in a way her aunt would surely not approve of, but I had no strength to pull away. When she finally did, we laughed lightly at ourselves, and I moved onto the settee next to her.

'Nathan, I prayed that this would happen, but I would not entice you. It had to be your decision.'

I said nothing, content to hold her. Relief flooded through my body that I had not lost her. I had come so close.

'I hope your regiment will not be too disappointed,' she said and kissed me on the cheek.

My heart dropped, but still I couldn't speak.

'Will we go to your father's?'

She carried on, but the words were unintelligible to my clouded brain. Finally, I blurted her name, and she looked at me in confusion.

'Betsey, I am not resigning my position.'

She made to pull away, but I held tightly.

'Don't you see? We can be happy together for as long as possible, and I will come back to you.'

Her brows pulled together, and her face flamed with anger

and embarrassment.

'I do not agree to those terms, as you well know.' She stood and moved to the other side of the room, putting as much space as possible between us.

'Would you leave me alone, possibly with a child on the way, while you go off to war? Your promise to return means nothing. What if I am left a widow? What if the war carries on for years as the last one did? You have already had my answer. How dare you attempt to trick me!'

'No, Betsey,' I begged. 'I meant no dishonesty.' I tried to approach her, but she swung away angrily with tears streaming down her face. 'I love you, and I know that you love me.'

'I do love you,' she said in a quietly fuming voice. 'You have the right of that. It is your own love that is in question, and you have confessed now twice where your true loyalty lies.'

She was gone in a swirl of skirts and cries that left me utterly devastated.

# Chapter 25
# New London – September 1775

*You will never know how much it has cost my generation to preserve your freedom. I hope you will make a good use of it.* – John Adams

I thought of Betsey's lack of enthusiasm for my last achievement as Colonel Webb presented me with my promotion to captain. We were preparing for the march to Cambridge, and I was struggling with the idea of leaving things so unsettled between Betsey and me.

What could I say? Her response would be to say that she had made herself entirely clear. She had. I had made my choice. Therefore, why did I still feel certain that things were unfinished? Was it because I was making the wrong choice? I wished Enoch or Ben were here to talk to, but each of them was attending to their duties and would likely tell me to do the same.

Busyness kept me from dwelling upon my problems of the heart. As recruits flooded into town, so came illness and infighting. From dawn until late into the night, I was occupied with training new arrivals, securing supplies, and giving what comfort I could to those who suffered with sickness.

I was leaving the tent of one bedridden with fever when I saw Betsey timidly making her way through the camp, and I rushed to her.

'My dear, what are you doing here?'

My mind sorted through possible responses in the split second it took her to speak. Had she changed her mind? Had something terrible happened? What news might have arrived from Boston?

'I wanted to see you one last time.'

The way she said it sent my heart plummeting into my shoes. It was worse than I could have imagined.

'Do not put it that way,' I begged. '"Hear my soul speak. Of the very instant that I saw you, did my heart fly at your service."'

'Do not quote Shakespeare to me, Mr Hale. "Cupid is a knavish lad," and I have therefore learned not to put my trust in him.'

I swallowed hard, knowing not which part of her statement hurt worse. Mr Hale she called me, after lovingly whispering Nathan. I fought hot tears, unwilling to let her unman me.

'I have brought some supplies as I've heard there is great need,' she said as though there was nothing more between us than residence in the same town.

I cleared my throat and took the proffered basket. 'There is. Accept my gratitude on the men's behalf.' Her eyes examined my face as if she wondered if I might say more. 'You have always shown me the greatest generosity and kindness since my arrival.'

Between us were the memories of laughter, shared dreams, and warm kisses.

'God go with you, Nathan,' she whispered.

I knew not what to say, but it was too late. She was walking away.

The next day, those who were healthy enough to walk were ordered into formation, and we began the march toward Cambridge, Massachusetts.

# Chapter 26
# Cambridge – October 1775

*Expectation is the root of all heartache.* – William Shakespeare

The arduous march had not kept my mind sufficiently occupied, and it was as if Betsey were constantly at my side, reminding me that I had abandoned her. I prayed that I had made the right decision. I begged God to keep her safe . . . and to help her wait. Despite all she had said, I thought she would.

Life in camp was another matter. I was once again caught up in duties of training men and the endless hunt for supplies. Many fell ill as men from across the region were brought together into the crowded accommodations. In the evenings, once my regular duties were as complete as they would be for that day, I occupied myself with visiting those who were sick and praying for their comfort and healing. Perhaps I thought this penance would cause God to nudge Betsey's heart in my direction.

Conversation around Cambridge was darker than that in New London. We had only imagined what was going on around Boston and said our fine pledges of liberty and freedom. Here, they had experienced the closure of their port, the invasion of redcoats, and bloody fighting.

'They do not even respect our dead,' one man had announced to those of us gathered at a local tavern. 'Steal bodies from graves just to desecrate them, they do,' he said before swallowing half of his ale in one gulp. 'Run you through with their bayonet whether you're alive or dead, they will. . . love those bayonets, they do,' he ended in a low murmur.

I did not remain long in the tavern, for it was doing little to lift my spirits. When I returned to camp, I saw tents being raised at the outer edge and assumed we had new arrivals.

Will Hull came up next to me. Finding him here had been one of the few happy occurrences since arriving. We had reminisced of our Yale days as if they were decades past and reassured ourselves that we far outshined the Harvard men who here surrounded us.

'For smallpox quarantine,' he said, indicating the tents that were going up. 'General says the pox is more likely to kill us than the British.'

I shivered to think of one ending their life that way instead of in battle. What a waste.

I had to turn away from the sight of those tents and the doom within them. One in three who caught the pox died of it, and it claimed young and old alike. It was more than I could think about on top of the duties already on my shoulders. I could only pray that God would give them peace in the midst of their suffering.

Will was talking, so I tried to focus on his words and forget the pox. Cannon fire boomed in the near distance, and I was getting used to pretending that none of us feared it.

'We should send out some men for firewood. It is pleasant today, but we both know how quickly that can change this time of year.'

I agreed and assigned the task to a few new recruits who were unlucky enough to be nearby.

'One would think those redcoats had endless ammunition,' Will groaned while rubbing his temples. 'They are trying to force us into submission by irritation.'

I chuckled half-heartedly. The cannon kept me slightly off

balance – not thinking quite straight – just as I knew it was meant to do, but I was ashamed to admit it. We made our way through camp. The presence of officers kept fighting and gambling at a minimum, and I had little else to do at the moment. No one tells new soldiers how much boredom they will endure.

The next day was worse for it had rained through the night, so rivulets of mud ran down the worn paths between the tents. I couldn't help but think that our number of those fallen ill would increase with this cold and filth.

I huddled up with Will around a small campfire where we attempted to warm some biscuits. I missed the Richards' table and the company I had shared there.

We forced the men through drills in the rain and mud. We would be no good to Washington if we only knew our task when warm and cheered by sunshine. It was miserable work, and I knew my uniform would never be its original white again. However, I was proud of the men who neither complained nor reduced their efforts.

We fell into a routine of drilling, eating, sleeping – all with British cannon blasting in the background. One day, a cow was killed by one of their cannonballs, so we took the afternoon to butcher and cook the meat. The redcoats had gifted us with a fine feast.

It was hard to believe that months had gone by since that New London town meeting when I had stood and offered to lead the march. I still hadn't seen fighting, was still drilling and waiting. And I had left Betsey behind for this.

I was greatly cheered when I saw a familiar face strolling through camp.

'Joseph!'

He turned toward me and broke into a wide grin as he rushed forward.

'Brother! You look well.'

Joseph looked me up and down as he made this proclamation, and I could imagine Enoch interrogating him regarding my condition when he returned home.

'It is wonderful to see you. What brings you here?'

I might have been worried that he brought bad tidings, but Joseph was ever one to wear his heart on his sleeve and I discerned no sorrow in his features.

'Father sent some supplies,' he said, taking a pack from his back and handing it to me.

'That was a kindness. Extend to him my gratitude.'

I hefted the bag and was impressed by its weight. My stomach grumbled in anticipation of what I might find inside.

'I have also been instructed to reassure you of our sisters' love,' Joseph recited dutifully, 'and that of several other village girls.'

I rolled my eyes and led him toward my tent.

'Let us find what cakes our sisters have sent to demonstrate their affection,' I said, indicating the pack.

'I think to enlist,' Joseph admitted once we were alone in my tent, the crumbs of Joanna's apple cake all that remained.

Not wanting to respond too quickly, I pressed my lips together and considered my brother. He was five years my elder but had long looked to Enoch and I for advice.

'What does father say?' I asked.

'It would be a hardship to lose my help on the farm,' he admitted, but then grew more animated. 'But your schoolhouse needed you, too, Nathan! And surely other homes and businesses needed all of the men here.' He gestured wildly to include, I assumed, all men currently serving in the militia.

It could not be denied, so I nodded but remained noncommittal.

'It must be your decision, Joseph. Neither father nor I can make it for you. Your life could be demanded for the cause, and only you can decide if you are willing to make that sacrifice.'

This sobered him. I could tell he was thinking of the way girls would admire his uniform more than he was considering conditions in camp or the chance that a musket ball might tear through his flesh.

He breathed in deeply before nodding in concession. 'I will think more on it, brother. You have the right of it.'

'I usually do.'

This earned me a punch on the arm as I knew it would, but there are some things a brother cannot resist.

I was sad to see Joseph leave the next day, though I tried not to let it show. It would do no good for a captain in the militia to become teary-eyed because he missed his family. Joseph was composing himself in a similar way, so we parted casually as men who had no fear that war could take one of us before we had the chance to reunite.

Joseph left with his bag filled with letters I had written to each family member. I had little news to share, but it helped me feel connected to them, and I longed for their replies.

When a packet of letters came for me, I tried to remain nonchalant until I was inside my tent. There, I tore into the pile, hoping for news from New London as well as Coventry.

'Gilbert Saltonstall,' I murmured to myself as I broke the letter's seal. 'What do you have to tell me.'

He shared news of his father's business and Stephen's desire to join me at Boston. He had been left behind to secure New

London's defenses.

Then came a line my mind refused to comprehend.

*Other gossip about town is that Elizabeth Adams has become engaged to Thomas Poole.*

I read it and reread it, begging the words to form into something else.

'Betsey?'

I was embarrassed by the whiney childlike tone of my voice and the hot tears that sprang to my eyes, although nobody was present to witness either.

Gil said only that he knew Betsey and I had both resided with the Richards and been acquainted, but he knew better than that. I wasn't sure if I appreciated him breaking the news as if it would not rend my soul or if I resented it. The letter remained unfinished atop those I hadn't even opened.

I flung open the flap door of my tent and stormed out of camp, none daring to inquire of my destination. My heart raged inside my chest as I climbed a hill in the chill air, and I happily invited the physical strain to replace the emotions I knew not how to cope with.

Somehow a memory of Yale surfaced in my mind as the wind tore my hair from its tie and salt air stung my face. We had been discussing *Paradise Lost* for the Linonia Society, and Ben had surprised us all by claiming to understand Satan's furious reaction to the love between Adam and Eve. How could he, a preacher's son at that, have compassion for the fallen angel in his battle against God and his creation?

'Can you not feel his envy?' Ben had asked, leaning forward with passion in his eyes. 'That "heavenly love" found "outside carnal pleasure" – it is beyond his reach. He sees what he can never have, so he seeks to destroy it.'

We had shaken our heads at Ben then and moved on, but now I wondered what he had experienced that gave him such insight into the devil's jealousy for my own eyes had been opened.

Reaching the crest of the hill, a forceful gust of wind almost knocked me off my feet. My face was becoming chapped, but it could not compare with the pain coursing through my very veins.

Had I not thought she meant it? She had given me months to change my mind – had offered one last opportunity before I left. But I had convinced myself that she would wait, that she would submit to my will.

I screamed, and my sorrow was carried off by the wind to where God alone heard it.

# Chapter 27
# Cambridge – November 1775

*Wherefore, my beloved brethren, let every man be swift to hear, slow to speak, slow to wrath; for the wrath of man worketh not the righteousness of God.* – James 1:19-20

I had wanted to come here to see something extraordinary. Now that curiosity was satisfied, and I longed for New London – as it had been, not as I would find it were I to return today. I had flattered myself that I would find glory and then have my happiness with Betsey, for I had neither.

Rain had been replaced with snow that blew in through tent flaps and froze us in our beds. Supplies were scarce, and we had begun slaughtering horses in order to have meat. Nothing was as I had expected to find it, and I still had not proven myself against the enemy.

My steps were meant to take me to evening prayer, but I had no heart for it. Not that it was God's fault I had made a mess of things, but I could not hear the words of love and forgiveness. I could not sit still to listen. I walked instead toward Prospect Hill where wagers were often laid on wrestling matches and other feats of strength and agility among the bored and frozen men.

I could hear Enoch's voice in my head, reprimanding me for my missed devotions, but he was soon drowned out by the sounds of men cheering or booing as their chosen man won or lost ground.

My cold fingers fumbled at the buttons of my waistcoat as I approached the crowd circling the makeshift ring, and I signaled the rough-looking man organizing the contests that I wished to be paired.

The one selected as my opponent was well matched in terms of height and build, but I knew as I stepped toward him that I brought greater passion with me to this fight. He was here for the recreation. I had Satan's desire to destroy. His good-natured grin disappeared when he met my eye, but it was not enough.

His slow movements were easy to counter, and I slammed his body to the ground as if Thomas Poole possessed him and I could steal his fiancé if I won. We grasped and grappled on the ground, the mud seeping into my mouth and ears. I roared with anger and shoved him beneath me with such force that I heard the crowd gasp. Then I held him like the devil I had convinced myself he was until two men pulled me up, yelling that he couldn't breathe.

The poor bloke was spluttering and spitting mud when the redness left my vision and I shook my head to clear it. Dismayed at my actions as my blood cooled, I approached him with my hand extended.

'I owe you an apology. It is the redcoats I wish to kill, not you.'

He glared at me and blew mud and snot out of his nose, barely missing my feet. Then the tension left his stance, and he took my hand.

'Tis alright. We'll get them together one day soon, we will.'

I nodded, dissatisfied that this was where my patriotic principles had led me. Releasing his hand, I pressed my lips firmly together as all the angry steam vented out of me. I promised myself I would henceforth act the officer I was, not like some raw minuteman. I returned to my tent and wrote letters to Betsey that I would never send.

Outside, the rain began to fall.

The next morning, I could smell the mud and worse before I rose from where I was huddled under my covers. My breath frosted in the air, and I was not eager to leave my warm cocoon. Familiar voices filtered through the tent walls, so I forced myself into action, not wishing to be out of uniform when the men arrived. I was shrugging into my coat when they called my name from just outside the tent.

'What is it?' I asked, stepping out into the grey day.

'They won't pay our wages, sir. Men are preparing to leave. They'd rather go home and have nothing than stay here and starve.'

I nodded but would not join them in justifying actions of possible deserters. We all had reasons for no longer wishing to be here.

'Lead the way, if you would.'

They traipsed through the mucky paths. I never thought I would be thankful for colder weather, but a good freeze would harden the ground and lessen the foul stink that rose from it.

We arrived at a tattered tent where two men stood guarding the entrance with what I thought was a silly amount of self-importance. Yet, they were braving the elements and doing their duty, so I nodded to them each as I ducked inside.

Voices clamored for attention and increased in volume once they realized an officer had arrived to judge the situation. I held up a hand to silence them before indicating that those who had brought me here should begin.

'These two here were headed for home, they were,' the first explained, pointing at the only men present with packs secured to their backs.

'But we knew what the general thinks of deserters, so we brought them here,' added another.

By 'the general,' of course, he meant Washington. I knew not how many generals served in the Continental Army, but the general was always Washington.

The captives held their peace no longer.

'We are starving, sir! How must it be for our families?'

'We have not been paid for months. How are we to live off nothing, and have nothing to send home?'

My hand silenced them again, but I nodded my understanding. Gazing around the tent, I wondered how many others had considered leaving. Had they convicted these two out of devotion to the cause or envy that they had not been brave enough to leave themselves?

I pulled out the little book that was always in my jacket pocket. Here I recorded the payments I made to the men, requests I made for supplies, and other bits of daily information. The men quieted as even those who couldn't read peered forward trying to determine what I meant to do.

'Men, I understand your concerns but cannot condone desertion. I am willing to share my own wages, such as they are, among you for the sake of your families and our cause.' I stopped myself before I could add that I had no family waiting for me or my income and little hope for one in the future. Their eyes lit up, assuaging my personal pain the tiniest amount.

As I moved to record the names and calculate how much I could give them, the men seemed humbled.

'We can't let you do that, sir.'

'Wouldn't be right.'

'You shame us, sir.'

That hadn't been my intention, but I wasn't sure what to

say. Their protests rumbled around the room until heads bobbed in agreement.

'We won't take your money, captain.'

I smiled weakly at them, in sudden wonder that loyalty still existed in the world. Nodding, I put my book away.

'Nothing is as we expected it would be,' I said, and they murmured their agreement, 'but I am going to do whatever it takes to get you men the supplies you need, even if I can't do much to collect your pay.'

'We appreciate you doing what you can, sir,' said a man who, to my knowledge, had not yet spoken. He held out his hand, apparently on behalf of them all, and I took it.

With one last glance around the dark tent, I tipped my head to them before leaving, wondering as I did so if they would all stay. The war had barely begun. What would happen if we couldn't convince people to keep fighting it?

I was considering how to best make a case for the men to my superior officers as I strode through camp when a young man almost ran into me. He looked too exuberant to be apologetic as he yelled, 'Congress has declared independence!'

He kept running, so I had no chance to ask where his news had come from. I hoped it was true and that it would buoy the men's spirits even if it couldn't fill their bellies.

In the coming days, no corroborating reports arrived regarding our supposed independence. We whined and complained about what could be taking congress so long. Those conversations inevitably disintegrated into liturgies on the many failings of congress and our continued lack of supplies and pay.

I had gone as high as General Israel Putnam with my concerns about the conditions and the men's likelihood of desertion, but his hands seemed to be as firmly tied as my own. Encouraging my men to forage and hunt to fill their pots, I despaired of what other steps I might take.

A mission to complete was an ideal distraction from our complaints and boredom, so I was pleased to have an assignment although it was one that I would have disdained during those idyllic days at New London.

We were to scatter beyond the edge of camp to chase away redcoats that were stealing our cattle. The men were keen on this less than heroic duty and eager to protect what little sustenance we had. Therefore, my regiment and I prepared to move out and protect the cows.

Little coverage was provided by the barren landscape, so we crawled through tall grass and used trees and boulders as far as they went. A small boat of British troops had been dragged up the beach at Lechmere Point, the same spot the bastards had landed to march on Lexington and Concord, but they got not nearly so far this time.

The redcoats had come prepared for thievery rather than fighting and were quickly repelled by a few shots from the men who first spotted them. My men laughed as the enemy hightailed it for their boat, but I was disappointed that we failed to take any captives or reduce their numbers for the next time we might meet.

At least we still had our cows.


A dark cloud loomed over our camp the next day, and I felt as though my own mood had summoned it. Betsey had haunted my dreams and mocked my duty to live in the mud and protect livestock instead of marrying her and raising strong sons. It was the accuracy of her observations that angered me more than anything else. I had lost her and gained nothing.

Through the frigid gloom of our camp, I made my way to the clearing where the Word was daily preached. I was in need of a healthy dose and wished Enoch was at my side to hear it. I longed for a future with Betsey, but it was Enoch's absence felt sharply today. How had we believed we might move on separately after spending our whole lives together?

I sighed as I took a place near the front. By myself.

The preacher knew his audience was filled with weary, desperate men. Appropriately, he skipped the opening joke or witty story that some reverends used to warm the congregation. I thought Ben's father probably started sermons that way. But this man didn't. He dug right in, and I was glad.

'For how can I endure to see the evil that shall come unto my people? Or how can I endure to see the destruction of my kindred?'

He quoted this scripture and pinned us with his bright cerulean eyes, drawing us all in.

'I know you boys recognize these words from Esther, but the Lord means them for you too. Today. Now.'

He nodded, satisfied that he had adequately emphasized that point.

'What Esther did was give everything she had to serve her people. Her country.'

He nodded more vigorously this time as he looked around and challenged us all to do our duty as well as this ancient woman had.

'She - a mere woman! She was willing to sacrifice herself for the sake of her people. Can we as men fail to do the same? What have we endured that we cannot suffer for the sake of our mothers, wives, and daughters?'

This time he shook his head to indicate that we had no

sufficient answers to this rhetorical inquiry.

As he continued talking about Esther and what she had been willing to risk, I felt my spirit refresh. The weight on my shoulders felt lighter than it had since receiving the fateful letter. Perhaps I was meant to focus on the duty to my country, at least for now, and leave my unknown future in God's trustworthy hands. Sadness still lingered deep in my chest, but I returned to my tent more secure in the fact that I was doing what I needed to do.

Will Hull met me at my tent. He shuffled and fidgeted impatiently. Before I could greet him, he grasped my arm and spoke in a low voice.

'Colonel Huntington has been given leave.'

He pulled me into my own tent as he said it, and I frowned as we faced each other in the dark.

'Didn't he just return?' I asked.

Will nodded and took a deep breath. 'His poor wife hanged herself after he left.'

'God have mercy.'

Neither of us spoke for a moment as we each considered the hardships that those outside of camp endured. We men assumed that no one suffered as we did, but what was it like for the women left at home?

'He said she has been delirious in her misery, but of course he couldn't have anticipated this.'

'No,' I whispered. 'I can't imagine what he's feeling.' Guilt. Embarrassment. Sorrow. Neither Will nor I would say any of these aloud, but somehow it made my own burden a bit lighter to know that I wasn't the only man carrying one.

# Chapter 28
# Cambridge – December 1775

*There is a price tag on human liberty. That price is the willingness to assume the responsibilities of being free men. Payment of this price is a personal matter with each of us.* – James Monroe

My head was throbbing when I awoke, and the image of Mrs Huntington's body swaying from the rafters was burned into the back of my eyes. But I was also more determined to fight and to win. It was the only way to make the sacrifices worthwhile. I could not lose Betsey and Jedediah lose his wife all for nothing.

If my sister was here, she would mix up a tonic of willow bark or feverfew. I wondered if I could find a remedy for my headache here where some lacked shoes and blankets. Closing my eyes, I determined prayer was my best chance and asked God to be merciful in how much suffering I must endure.

I reluctantly left the warmth of my bed to find some water and biscuits. When I swallowed the icy liquid, it burned down my throat. Worried that poor sleep was not my only ailment, I decided to ask around for some healing herbs. While I was on this mission, a boy came around with mail and handed me a letter.

It was from Elihu Marvin, and I shoved it in my pocket expecting that it held little news that couldn't wait until I was back in my private quarters, such as they were. I had been offered a weak willow bark brew and wished to drink it before it cooled.

As I drained my cup and returned it to my benefactor, I realized that I had not yet seen Will this morn, so I made my way to his tent. The flap was closed, and no sound came from within.

'Will?' I hailed without peeking inside to help preserve whatever warmth he had managed to trap within. He did not answer, but I thought I perceived some sound.

I quickly ducked inside, opening the entrance as little as possible. Will was still up to his nose in covers with an arm thrown across his eyes. He groaned at my approach.

'Are you poorly, my friend,' I foolishly asked. 'A man has some willow bark. Shall I get him to brew some for you?'

In a scratchy voice, Will whispered, 'That would be good of you.'

I assured him I would quickly return, and, forgetting about my own minor ailment, I rushed back out to find comfort for my friend. This time, I had to barter for the willow bark, my source having suddenly realized its value, but I soon had a cup in hand and strode to deliver it to Will while it was still warm and soothing.

He did not try to sit up but let me prop up his head so that he could slurp the tonic before drifting back to sleep. I knelt and offered prayer for his healing and tried not to think how miserable the camp conditions were for one in need of a warm fire, good food, and a sweet woman to provide nurturing. I thought of Eliza again and smiled when I pictured her doting over Will if we were home.

Longing for Coventry, my father's house, and the company of Enoch and Eliza washed over me like a tidal wave, and I determined then and there to request leave. All this time I had been here accomplishing little. Surely, I had earned some time to check on my family while the armies hibernated in winter camps.

Leaving Will to his rest, I returned to my tent to write my request. Then I remembered Elihu's letter in my pocket. I tore it open, anticipating inane daily news, which is what made up most of it, but I was brought up short when I reached Betsey's name.

It took me a moment to realize that it was indeed her name, for Elihu mentioned Mrs Poole, a woman with whom I did not believe myself acquainted. When he went on to say that she had 'desired me to enclose a letter from her,' I had searched my brain more thoroughly to connect my sweet Betsey with this matronly Mrs Poole.

My heart felt as though someone had speared it through and flung it to the ground.

She was married. Elihu apologized for his failure to obtain the letter from her before sending off this missive, and I wondered what she had wanted to say to me. What could she say? She was Mrs Poole now.

I tossed aside my friend's letter and took up my request for leave. I would go home and take comfort in the company of my loving family, for Betsey was truly lost to me forever.

When I delivered my request to my commanding officer, I discovered a familiar face among others with their own business.

'Stephen,' I called, happy to find another friend at camp.

The confusion on his face broke into a broad grin when he saw me. 'Secundus!' He looked around as if in wonder to find me without my brother at my side, despite our time in New London. I must confess it still shocked me at times as well.

'I did not know you had arrived,' I admitted shaking his hand. 'It is good to see you.'

'The circumstances could be better,' he said with a laugh.

'We've endured worse....'

'The dining hall!'

I was thankful that he did not mention Betsey, and we chatted for a few moments before I said that I was there to request leave.

'When I return, I will find you straight away.'

We agreed that the winter would pass more agreeably in the company of friends, and I was pleased to have both Will and Stephen near. I thought of Ben and my brother, but one must not be choosey about the blessings God sends.

Will did not appear to have shifted an inch since morning, so I once again left him to sleep with the intention of bringing him another willow bark brew later. I would make sure Stephen knew of Will's need if he were not better before I journeyed home. We Yale men must look out for one another, after all.

Returning to my own tent, I retrieved Elihu's letter from where I had dropped it. He, like many of my other friends, bemoaned my lack of letter writing. They were all correct in their accusations, but what did I have to write about in this dismal place? However, Elihu wrote of his throat distemper, which made my own throat itch in sympathy, and workaday affairs, so surely I could do the same.

Determined to be a better friend, I took out fresh sheets of paper and wrote almost identical missives to Elihu, Ben, and Enoch. I told them of finding Stephen and Will at camp but little of the deprivation and illness we strived to avoid. I made no mention of Betsey. What could I say?

The letters posted, I obtained a tonic from the physician for Will and walked toward his tent as the sun sank below the horizon. The cold deepened and the sky darkened as I hurried my pace across the frozen, rutted path.

The sight of four men sitting around a makeshift table outside surprised me, for it was so cold that most took refuge in their tents. As I approached them, playing cards were scooped up and tucked into sleeves.

Heat rose to my face. 'Are we gentlemen and soldiers here or heathen no better than any redcoat?'

None of them met my eye or responded aloud.

'Vices such as this are to be shunned, as you well know,' I added, daring any of them to challenge a captain. I spotted a card they had missed and picked it up. One of them looked about to object, but he stopped himself when I raised an eyebrow in his direction.

The card tore easily into a dozen pieces which I threw back at them. 'Pray that you are no longer drawn to such sin,' I ordered as I shooed them away.

They grumbled but not loud enough for my ear to catch their words, and I watched to ensure that they dispersed before continuing on to Will's tent.

'Any better, friend?' I asked in what I hoped was a soothing voice as I entered. He murmured an unconvincing response, and I took my seat next to him.

'Here, this will help.' Again, he only let me prop him up slightly to swallow the tonic. He seemed exhausted by the effort. 'Perhaps, I should bring the physician tomorrow.'

I was worried that his needs exceeded the care I was providing, and I wished Eliza was here to tell me what to do. How did women always know what to do when one was ill?

Will was asleep again, so I asked God to bless him and left him to his rest.

The next morning, I received approval for my leave and recruited assistance in Will's care. He was no better, but the physician seemed unconcerned after his examination. With the threat of smallpox, everything else was considered a minor ailment, so I was thankful that was not Will's diagnosis.

I tried to place my friend's fate in God's hands and not worry, but I was grateful to have found Stephen. He offered his hand to help Will, though he was no better suited to the task than myself. It made me wonder what chores women at home were forced to attend to that were beyond their normal realm. What would we all be like when this war ended? It didn't seem that we could simply go back to the way things had been before, but those were concerns for another time and I had enough worries for today.

It was a welcome sight when I entered Will's tent on the fifth day and he was sitting up waiting for me. This was such an improvement that I felt my icy skin crack with the broadness of my grin.

'Well, good morn, Will! You're awake.'

He nodded sheepishly, and I understood. It was difficult to know you had lain there helpless for days dependent on others.

'Do you crave something? You must be famished.'

At this he laughed. He had not been ill enough to forget that there were no well-stocked pantries for me to raid on his behalf.

'Anything you can find is appreciated, Nathan,' he said in a still scratchy voice. 'I've never been hungrier.'

'My mother would say that's a good sign of healing. I'll not tarry,' I assured him as I went back out into the cold.

Thankfully, a cart of supplies had been recently delivered, so I was able to secure some good bacon, biscuits, and even a dram of rum for Will. I hurried through the frigid wind, careful not to twist my ankle on the frozen, uneven path.

Arriving somewhat breathless, I proudly held out my offering. Will smiled, though he still looked exhausted, and I split the rations into small meals for him to have throughout the day, knowing it wouldn't take much for him to feel full and sleepy.

'Thank you, Nathan,' he murmured as he sipped the rum after filling his belly. 'You are a true friend.'

I patted his arm and left him to rest, feeling better about packing to travel home now that Will was on the mend.

Snow swirled through the air and made the frozen mud slippery and treacherous. A dull ache began in the back of my head, and I was reminded that I also had not regained my full health. Rest and good food were easier obtained at home. All I had to do was get there.

It was a long way to travel by foot, and I sure did miss my horse, but that was the only way to go. I put on my thickest socks and patched a hole in my boot. My ration of bacon was wrapped and tucked into my pack. Little else was necessary for my trip.

I checked on Will one more time and was pleased to find Stephen at his side.

'I'm off then,' I announced unnecessarily, for they could see I was bundled up and carried my pack.

'God go with you, Nathan,' Stephen said, rising and grasping my hand.

'And may he keep you both well.' I leaned over to pat Will on the shoulder, nodded to them both, and left the relatively warm tent for the cold road that would be my only companion for the next several days.

# Chapter 29
# Coventry – December 1775

*He heals the broken in heart and binds up their wounds.* – Psalm 147:3

The first day had not crushed my spirits. Thoughts of home kept me moving steadily as the snowdrifts deepened and the temperatures plunged. However, by the third day, my head pounded and one of my ankles ached. I sniffled through a frozen, red nose and longed for home like never before.

I felt like a little boy on Christmas morning when my father's big, red barn came into view through the blowing snow. In fact, I had missed Christmas by a day and was stumbling up to the porch on December twenty-sixth. When the door opened, revealing my grinning brother and a warm hearth glowing behind him, I felt tears prick at the corners of my eyes.

Enoch's arms wrapped around me, and the warmth of his embrace almost undid me. I had only arrived, but I was already wondering how I would ever leave.

More siblings surrounded me. My pack was pulled from my back, and hands touched my arms and back as if to reassure my family that I was truly present. I squeezed my eyes shut as they murmured around me and feeling flowed back into my chilled limbs.

'Thanks to God for your safe arrival,' Enoch declared.

One of my younger brothers was less impressed. 'Nathan, you look awful!'

Everyone laughed and ushered me further in so that the door could be closed on the cold out of doors. A warm brew of local herbs was thrust into my hands as a thousand questions were asked of me at once. They all quieted as my father entered the room.

He stepped forward with his face stony, and I recognized the signs of a man trying not to show too much emotion. His eyes took in my uniform, my thin frame, my wind chapped skin. He blinked quickly and a vein stood out in his neck as he struggled for control. Then he broke into a smile and moved toward me with his arms held wide.

'My boy,' he cried and held me tightly.

When he released me, we had all shed a few tears and laughed at each other. Conversation flowed all around me, and I took comfort in being home.

Waking with a sore throat and aching head was not so worrisome within the warm house and with Joanna to nurse me back to health. Enoch sat at my bedside. We had much on which to catch each other up. I could almost forget that I was ill in the atmosphere of pleasant coziness.

As Enoch talked about his studies with Reverend Huntington and upcoming exam to receive his preaching license, I wondered how different my life might have been had I returned to our father's homestead. It wasn't a realistic consideration. In a family of eight sons, we couldn't all remain home. Enoch, too, would leave soon enough once he was assigned to a congregation.

After a few days at home, I could hold back my confession no longer. Enoch and I were alone, and I knew he had been patiently waiting for me to share the burden on my heart, which he could see as clearly as if I carried it in a haversack.

'I have lost Betsey.'

I expected lightning to flash and thunder to crash, but the apocalyptic statement was met by silence.

'I feared as much,' Enoch said in a low, comforting voice. 'I am so sorry, Nathan.'

He made no promises about the healing of my heart and asked for no details of how it had been broken. Enoch simply waited for me to say whatever I needed to say.

'It is my fault,' I admitted. 'She wanted to marry me, and I rejected her.'

Saying it aloud in front of the one person on earth I could be entirely honest with broke my floodgates. I sobbed as I could not remember ever doing before, my body shaking with the harshness of it and my head aching as tears ran in rivulets down my cheeks.

'Dear brother,' Enoch whispered. He knelt beside the bed and held me like I was a child. He did not ask for explanation of what must seem like an incredible story. He murmured soothingly until I gained control, and then he rose to fetch a cool drink.

After a few moments, I muttered in a raspy voice, 'Nothing is as we planned.' I sniffed and looked around the simple room. 'We spoke boldly of philosophy and freedom, but the reality is harsh and ignoble.'

Enoch nodded, and, though he was home not facing the same hardships I had faced, I was sure he understood.

'You will make a good minister.'

He smiled. 'God is good.' He examined my bloodshot eyes and starved body. 'He might not seem so now, but He has plans for you too.'

I frowned. Once I would have easily agreed. Had we been naïve? Or had I become cynical and selfish?

'Not every man would make the sacrifices you are willing to

make, Nathan. Our country will not survive if we lack men like you.'

Three of our brothers were planning to join regiments, but not Enoch. I was glad. It was enough that one of us went. He could remain free of visions of war and serve a higher calling.

I didn't know what else to say now that I had broken down. I looked at my brother with hopelessness.

'Would you like to tell me about it?' he asked softly, and suddenly I realized I did.

Enoch stayed by my side for hours as I poured it all out. Betsey. The conditions at camp. How often I missed him. I did not cry again but felt a deep cleansing of my soul by sharing my burdens with my brother.

# Chapter 30
# Coventry – January 1776

*The truth is, all might be free if they valued freedom and defended it as they aught.* - Samuel Adams

My first mission of the new year was recruiting some men to my regiment. Finally feeling up to the task, I left the warmth of my father's home to visit some of my childhood friends. This changing world made it feel as though a lifetime had passed since I had seen some of them.

I could now borrow my father's sleigh, so my journey was easier than it had been when I left camp. I came to the drive leading to the Wright farm and turned toward the house. Within, I hoped to see Asher, a boyhood friend of mine. Based on the reports of my siblings, I expected to find him keen to join the patriotic cause.

The homestead was smaller than my father's and more ramshackle. It made me wonder if Asher's father could cope with his absence, but their struggle would not be unique at this time when so many men were away from their farms and businesses. I could not allow this concern to turn me from my objective.

Before I had reached the door, Asher opened it to welcome me inside. He had the look of one fresh from bed with mussed hair and disheveled clothes but a bright, cheery countenance. I gladly took the offered seat near the fire and inquired as to his family's health and well-being before sharing my proposal.

'I am in need of a waiter, one to help with daily tasks and the organization of the regiment. I'll not withhold anything from you. It is also my duty to recruit more men before my return to camp.'

He sighed and sat back thoughtfully, and I appreciated that he was not too quick to respond. It was not a decision to be made impetuously. I waited while the fire crackled.

'I am of a mind to join you, Nathan. It is only that I worry for my father, but I am sure that some leave family in more precarious situations that his.'

I nodded. It was true. I thought of Colonel Huntington's wife and suppressed a shiver.

Asher slapped his knees and stood as if movement was required to make up his mind with certainty.

'I shall return with you, Nathan. Can I call myself a patriot while I hide safely at home? And the opportunity to serve alongside a friend is not likely to come twice.'

I held my hand out to him as I stood. 'It means more to me than you know. Having trusted men at my side is more important than anything right now.'

His grip was firm and his face serious. I had chosen well.


Asher and I spent several days traversing the countryside and recruiting those we most wished to join us and some we might not have preferred but were keen to do their part. It would take all kinds of people and sacrifices before this conflict ended. The time passed quickly, and too soon it was time to return to camp with my group of recruits.

Although it would be easier to travel with company, my throat threatened to close at the thought of leaving my family again. I said a private farewell with Enoch, thanking him for all he had done - all he was - for me. He shrugged as if it was nothing, but I knew he had pulled me from the pit.

The rest of the family gathered on the porch to wave goodbye as I and my recruits marched away, not knowing if or when we might return.

As soon as we arrived in camp, we began to hear murmurs of General George Washington's arrival. Will Hull found me, and I was thankful that he appeared hale and healthy. He quickly informed me that Washington had rearranged regiments into cohesive units, his goal creating unity among men who tended to demonstrate loyalty to their home state rather than congress. It was a good idea, and I was glad to hear that Will had requested to remain in my regiment.

With Asher, Will, and Stephen, I was almost content or could at least set aside the thoughts of those I missed for a while. We stowed Asher's few belongings inside my tent and made to hunker down for the long, cold winter.

# Chapter 31
# Cambridge – February 1776

*The cause of America is in great measure the cause of all mankind.*
– Thomas Paine

Winter camp is not for the weak of heart – or one who is weak in any way. We were cold and hungry but still had to endure drilling and foraging duty. If it weren't for the presence of friends and frequent letters from others, I might have despaired.

I felt guilt when I sent thin, shivering men out to forage, so I often went along to share in their misery. It was necessary to cast our net further out as the fields and homesteads closest to our camp were stripped of all that was useful. We might have created some new Tories with our requisitioning. Each night during my prayers, I repented that I had promised good people that payment would be forthcoming when I doubted the truth of it.

With the early dark and frigid weather, we tended to gather around fires in the evening or huddle in our tents with low candles burning. We passed around newspapers and letters, trying to figure out what was happening in the world outside our struggle to survive.

A book began to appear in camp to great acclaim. I had never heard of Thomas Paine, but as soon as I read his *Common Sense*, I wished Ben and Enoch were with me. Instead, I had to be content with letters to them asking for their thoughts and sharing my favorite lines.

Ought we to at this point declare an independency? I believed so but was so used to discussing these things with my

Linonian brothers that I waited anxiously for their replies.

Men in camp no longer asked, 'Common Sense, have you seen it?' They demanded, 'What think you of Common Sense?' One was a leper if you had failed to read it. Those who could not read were quick to quote the best lines they had heard others sharing.

Upon initial reading, it had been shocking when Paine insisted that 'there is something exceedingly ridiculous in the composition of monarchy.' However, now the line was often repeated throughout camp without concern of who might be listening. It may seem silly that those of us who bore arms against our king still felt a thrill at publicly speaking in opposition of him.

When a letter arrived from Enoch, I was unsurprised that he had been impressed with Paine's theories on the equality of man. Did God place greater value on King George than the nameless patriot? Enoch thought not.

Ben agreed that it was time that we thought of ourselves not as British colonists, but as Americans. He, of course, had put forth this idea long ago, before any of us had heard of Thomas Paine. I could see us sitting around the scarred table at Yale, discussing whether we were men of Connecticut, or in Ben's case New York, or America. We had already ceased thinking of ourselves as solely English.

Only with Stephen and Will could I discuss these things, and I allowed them the reading of my letters. We who had already signed up for service were, of course, of one mind when it came to independence, and believed along with Paine that it should be declared immediately.

We were a sad shadow of our Linonia days, squeezed together in a cold tent, thumbing through copies of Paine's pamphlet with numb fingers. However, our hearts and souls were the same, and we found a kindred spirit in the pages. Honor, virtue, and liberty – were these not the high ideals we had discussed for four years and strove toward now?

It became increasingly difficult to envision an outcome of reconciliation.

# Chapter 32
# New York City – March 1776

*It is really a critical Period. America beholds what she never did before.* – Nathan Hale

Our orders arrived to move to New York during spring's torrential rain season. We had survived winter's snow and cold, so I supposed our superiors believed us capable of any feat. Of course, most of the men were keen to prove it could be done rather than argue otherwise. Therefore, we packed our sodden gear and made our slippery way to the waiting boats.

I say we had battled through cold as though we now endured a warm spring shower, but that was not so. Temperatures had increased just enough for snow to become rain and the frozen mud to become a squelching mess. Our fingers and toes were still soon numb, and I shivered in my soaked wool coat.

Before we were all aboard the ships, I heard the angry murmuring of men who wondered why we would put such effort into the defense of New York City, a town that had seemed to embrace the British while Boston suffered at their hands. Maybe it was because of my friendship with Ben, but I was sure that New Yorkers were just as American as I was. Were there not Tories to be found in every colony? Yet each one must be defended as if we were completely united in purpose.

My comrades – Stephen, Will, and Asher – and I attempted to huddle together and stay warm as the transports were guided through the treacherous waves. It was hopeless as water seemed to find us from every direction. To distract each other, we spoke of home, but that soon grew depressing as we each wondered when we might see our families once again.

When the cliffs of Manhattan Island came into view, our spirits rose with the assurance that the place would be easily defended even against a greater force. Our boats took refuge in Turtle Bay, and I hoped to set my feet soon upon solid ground. I did not fear the raging waters, but I did not thrive upon the challenge as those made for seagoing did.

It made me think of Isaac. I could not recall when I had last heard from him, and I wondered if he had enlisted in his local regiment. My next letters to Ben and Elihu would have to include inquiries as to his well-being and whereabouts. Would asking about Betsey be improper? I had tried not to think about what message she had meant to send, for she now belonged to another.

During moments when the rain eased, I tried to make out more of the terrain along the shore. Among the reeds and rocks, I spotted a mansion high on a bluff with a glass greenhouse at its side. Before I could wonder about who lived in such an elaborate home, officers began shouting orders to prepare to disembark.

Though we were already soaked to the skin, we were thankful that the storm eased to a drizzle as we left the boats and unloaded our supplies. The shore was thick with mud, but the sun peeked out and began to warm the air.

We trudged through streets that quickly became ankle deep mud and looked for high ground upon which to set up tents. I was grateful to have quarters within a solid brick building, which Stephen and Asher were to share with me while Will roomed with other men from our regiment.

We laid out bedding to dry, and I had to resist the urge to lie down then and there. Little rest had been possible during the journey on the heaving ship, but I had duties to attend to before I could close my eyes. With a wistful glance back at our strewn about blankets, we left the room to see that our men were all housed and supplies all arrived.

The residents of New York did not welcome us. Women peeked at us through mostly closed curtains, and men openly glared as if daring us to challenge their loyalty. One spat in our direction, almost hitting my shoes, and we heard others mutter about yankees in their midst. I wondered not for the first time if we shouldn't leave these townies to their fate in the hands of the king's men.

The men of my regiment had their tents up and fires started, having made quick work of setting up camp. Only a few of the unwieldy pots that they were forced to carry were over fires since there was little available to put in them. More often, I saw them flipped over and used as stools or some such other use. If only congress had spent the money for those heavy pots on dried beef instead. It would have been of much greater use to us.

Having completed my inspection, I wearily returned to quarters that were warmed by a fire Asher had built. My blankets were dry, and I gathered them up eagerly. Before I could choose a spot to make by bed, Stephen pushed me toward the hearth.

'Stay warm, Nathan. I will sleep across the doorway.'

'You will be too cold, my friend,' I protested, thinking it was an unnecessary sacrifice, but Stephen was adamant. He was shaking his head before the words were out of my mouth.

'I shall not sleep otherwise,' he insisted, giving me another gentle shove in the direction of the warmer side of the room. Stephen checked that the door was secure and piled his bedding in front of it.

I smiled grimly, conceding to his wishes and feeling thankful to have such a friend with me.

When I awoke the next morning, my nose felt constricted with dust and filled with the scent of snuff that I had been too exhausted to notice the day before. I sneezed several times, but my roommates did not stir. Weak sunlight filtered through high windows and the air was thick with dust. Upon further inspection, I realized that the building must have been formerly used as a snuff mill, for the powdered remains clung to the walls and filled in the cracks between the floorboards.

Now that I knew it was there, it was as though I could feel the powder in my ears and throat as well as my nostrils. I began to cough and itch at my ears while my nose ran. With Stephen blocking the door, I couldn't escape to fresh air.

He and Asher began to stretch and groan as my theatrics disturbed their rest. A bit ashamed of myself, I sniffled and attempted to clear my throat and still my hands. When they too began to sneeze and cough, I felt a bit better.

We dressed quickly so that we could go outside. The air was fresh and crisp, and I was grateful that the sun promised a warmer, drier day. I was dreading a day of drilling and was therefore pleased to be assigned to lead a hunting expedition. My mouth watered at the thought of fresh venison as I selected men for the assignment.

After gathering supplies, we rowed over to Long Island, and I remembered Ben's tales of hunting near his Setauket home. Many Tories lived on the island, but we planned to stick to the woods and avoid confrontation with them. We pulled our boats onto the sand of a little cove and quietly entered the dark forest.

I could almost forget that we were an army taking on the power of Great Britain. Here, in the peaceful dimness with the smell of moss and pine in my nostrils, we were just men again, tracking deer as if to feed our family awaiting us at home.

I was reluctant to return to camp after our hunting expedition but hoped to be of greater worth to my country than I had so far proven to be. The bundles of meat we had secured and now loaded into our boats already seemed like a greater contribution than I had thus far provided, and I looked forward to presenting them to the men.

Stephen and I took the lead, shoving our boats away from shore and pointing them toward the southern tip of Manhattan. The water was calm and the breeze warm. Spring was, at last, overpowering the winter chill. I looked over at Stephen and saw his grin matched my own.

'How do you think Asher has enjoyed the drills?' he shouted across the low waves.

Poor Asher had been left behind with my other new recruits to learn the drills that the rest of us had been trudging through for months. He had not been happy with the separation but had understood that the training was necessary.

I laughed. 'We all must put in our time.'

Stephen nodded and squinted into the sun. As we rowed across the East River, I wondered about the fighting season that the warmer weather would bring.

It did not take long to arrive at the docks, where Asher and several others were ready to relieve us of our burden. My friend appeared more fit and firm thanks to the drills and in spite of the lack of good food. At least that problem was temporarily alleviated by the content of our boats.

'Nathan! You appear to have had good luck hunting,' Asher shouted as we tied off the boats.

'God has blessed our efforts,' I agreed.

'And we didn't miss a fortnight of drilling!' Stephen added, punching Asher lightly as he said it.

Asher took it good naturedly. It was one of the reasons I had asked him to be my waiter. He was not one to easily take offense and was good company. He laughed off the teasing and loaded up his arms with bundles of meat.

As we carried the packages to be distributed, Asher took a place alongside me. 'Someone has been looking for you.'

I had not a clue who he could mean, and he answered before I could ask.

'A Lieutenant Benjamin Tallmadge recently joined camp and asked to be informed as soon as you returned.'

'Ben!' I subconsciously increased my pace, but Asher kept up. 'He is a good friend from Yale,' I explained, realizing that Asher wouldn't know of Ben since he had rarely left Coventry previous to his current service.

'So he said,' Asher nodded. 'Seems a good sort.'

'The very best,' I agreed. I was eager to see my friend and discuss the everchanging world we lived in.

When I did see him, not an hour after my arrival, he embraced me warmly and it was as if not a moment had passed since we were last together. He looked as though the army uniform was designed specifically to suit his best features, and I asked what his father had thought of his enlistment.

Ben's face fell slightly, but he brightened quickly as he always did. 'He begged me to remain in my teaching position,' he admitted with a shake of his head. 'I cannot blame him for not being keen to have four sons at war, but a reverend must place his trust in providence as he urges the rest of us to do so.'

I pressed my lips together and thought of my own brothers. Four remained home with my father, but three others had joined up as I had.

'You are his prodigy – his favorite,' I teased, attempting to lighten the mood.

Ben smiled broadly. 'Of course, I am, and who could blame him?'

We laughed and moved on to less serious topics than fathers who fear the loss of their sons. I told him that hunting on Long Island was just as good as he had always claimed, and he nodded knowingly. He caught me up on news from friends and made me hope that a packet of letters awaited me at my quarters.

When I finally did seek out my bed that night, a few letters were there to greet me. I was too weary to read, but I had to at least peek at the one from Enoch before my candle burned out. He shared standard news that I skimmed over quickly. I stopped when I saw that my father had decided to build a new home. I lowered the letter and considered this and wondered how odd it would be to visit my family in a home I had never lived in.

'Not to worry, Eliza and Joanna have made papa promise to reuse the door with your tracing,' Enoch wrote in what I imagined was a joking tone. 'Of course, he will reuse all the doors to save on the cost of materials, but our sisters still feel they have won a victory.'

My candle sputtered, and I set the missive aside for a more careful reading the next day. I fell into an exhausted sleep as the dust of snuff tumbled through the air around me.

# Chapter 33
# New York City – May 1776

*The army is every day improving in discipline and it is hoped will soon be able to meet their enemy at any kind of play.* – Nathan Hale

The British were keen to prove that our ragtag army threatened them not one bit. Their ships sailed past just beyond cannon range with great frequency and sometimes even anchored in the East River as if to dare us to do something about it.

One day when a sloop was in the shadow of a larger warship near the Long Island shore, Asher pointed and shook his head.

'We ought not allow that!'

I shrugged, 'What can we do?'

'Teach them a lesson,' Asher insisted, and I just smiled. 'You don't think I'm serious?'

I looked at his earnest face and back at the sloop, and my smile faded as an idea began to form in my mind.

'How difficult would it be to row a flatboat over there under the cover of night?'

Now it was Asher who grinned. 'Ah, see. Now we're talking.' He rubbed his hands together eagerly and insisted he could easily accomplish the rowing.

'Not alone,' I said before his imagination could run away with him. 'Let us get Stephen and select a few others.'

I said no more because Asher had already strode off to fetch Stephen. Looking away from his retreating back, my eyes fixed upon our prize waiting just across the river. Low waves and warm sunlight created a glittering effect that was almost blinding, and I wondered how much moonlight there might be tonight.

I was thankful for the cover of clouds after the sun had set and the moon rose. We needed moonlight, but not too much. Six of us shoved off in a flatboat with linen tied around the oars. Slipping silently across the river, we listened for shouts of alarm that would force us to reverse our course.

None came.

We jumped when a voice called out in a London accent, 'All's well!'

A few nervous chuckles were silenced by my glare. They had not seen us, and there was no movement on the sloop. Had they left it unmanned due to its proximity to the larger ship? That seemed too easy. Perhaps everyone aboard was asleep, so little did they anticipate any action from us.

We swung our little boat alongside the sloop, and I think we were all a bit surprised to have made it this far. Two men were left to row it back, while the other four of us climbed over the edge, discovering two young men, boys really, sleeping on the deck.

Asher pulled the anchor while Stephen prepared to steer us back to camp and the rest of us held weapons ready.

The failed lookouts awoke first and realized their mistake. My heart softened at their bleary eyes and beardless chins. With my musket, I motioned for them to jump overboard. They took one wide-eyed look at each other and complied, though I wondered what welcome they would receive from their officers.

The movement of the boat and sound of footsteps must have alerted those below of something amiss. Three soldiers stormed up the ladder in various states of undress, but they were quickly taken captive and tied securely.

Once Asher had confirmed that no one else lurked below deck, we celebrated with whoops that echoed across the water and informed our two comrades in the flatboat of our success.

When we arrived at the dock, they had gathered a few others to help unload the supplies and escort the captives to General Putnam. For the first time since I left New London, I felt I was serving the purpose for which I had sacrificed so much.

# Chapter 34
# New York City – June 1776

*The Eyes of all our Countrymen are now upon us, and we shall have their blessings, and praises, if happily we are the instruments of saving them from the Tyranny mediated against them.* – George Washington

The loud knocking almost made Stephen jump out of his bedding, which he still carefully laid out across the threshold each night. Asher and I groaned to be so rudely awoken, but I was quickly more concerned with what had sent someone so urgently to our door with dawn barely broken.

It was not one visitor but two, and they practically shoved their way through the door once Stephen had opened it a crack.

Ben spoke quickly as Will nodded his support.

'A plot has been discovered,' he whispered, though there was none to overhear. 'A threat upon Washington's life.'

We became wide-eyed as schoolchildren as the realization of what the assassination of the general would do to the American cause.

'Men have been arrested,' Ben continued.

'One is a sergeant in Washington's own guard!' Will could hold back his voice no longer, and our eyes swiveled briefly to him in wonder. Those men were chosen specifically to secure Washington from such threats.

'It is said they planned to poison his food, but with a conspirator in his bodyguard corps they could have planned any number of possibilities,' Ben said, causing us all to turn back to him.

'How were they discovered?' Stephen asked, 'and are they sure they've got them all?'

Ben shrugged and answered only with what he had thus far learned. 'Some peas that had been served to the general were thrown to the chickens after he left them on his plate. Within hours, several of the chickens had died.'

I thanked God that Washington did not like peas and wondered if I would ever be able to eat them again.

Ben leaned in, and we all mirrored his movement. 'There are rumors that Washington was not the only target. Once they had removed him, they intended to turn their efforts to other generals in camp - Putnam and who knows who else.'

We were quiet for a moment, each wondering who would have led the army if this plot had been successful.

'There will be a court martial,' Will added quite unnecessarily, and we gazed at each other knowing what that would mean. A man, maybe several men, would hang.

The somber mood of our room continued when we went about camp. Men whispered and gave each other sidelong glances. Each wondered if more traitors were among us like slippery snakes in Eden.

I heard various tidbits - that the traitors were counterfeiting the new paper money, that they planned to spike our cannon, and even that they had hoped to turn New York over to the British with Washington's corpse swinging at the docks in welcome. The suggestion made me shiver despite the warm sun.

Rumors also swirled about regarding where the traitors were held. I supposed the general must wish to keep it a closely held secret to avoid any men taking justice into their own hands on his behalf. Washington would want things handled by the book to demonstrate the professionalism and effectiveness of his new army.

We had not long to wait. Within forty-eight hours, Sergeant Thomas Hickey had been convicted of treason and sentenced to hang. Thousands of us gathered in the region of the Bowery, though most could not possibly see or hear what occurred. My friends and I somberly waited for the man, who had posed as a brother in arms in order to betray us, to meet his doom.

The man dragged to the gallows was no longer wearing the blue coat and white breeches of Washington's guard. He looked curiously normal in cast-off clothing that fit ill his tall frame. This swarthy character would have seen any of us – all of us – die to please King George. It was a strange feeling to look upon him and to realize that, in a way, we were no better for we would kill any British soldier that crossed our path knowing nothing about what type of man he was.

Stepping up to the rope, Sergeant Hickey wiped his eyes. We weren't close enough to see his tears, but I prayed that it meant he was repentant as he went to his judgement. Even at war, I could not wish hell upon one who seemed so much like any one of us. I said as much to Ben.

'Is he grieved over what he has done or only sorrowful because of where it has ended?' he asked with a gesture toward the noose.

I shrugged. 'Thankfully, it is for God, not I, to decide.'

Ben nodded grimly with an almost imperceptible wince as Hickey's body swung.

# Chapter 35
# New York City – July 1776

*The Declaration of Independence, which had been solemnly adopted by Congress on the Fourth of July 1776, was announced to the army in general orders, and filled every one with enthusiastic zeal, as the point was now forever settled, and there was no further hope of reconciliation and dependence on the mother country.* - Benjamin Tallmadge.

When we next gathered together, it was for an entirely different purpose. The general had an announcement, and we were almost afraid to guess what it might be. We stood organized in regimental formation and looked little like the squeezed in mob that had witnessed the traitor's hanging.

Therefore, we appeared as a real army in brushed uniforms and stiff salutes when Washington stood on a balcony to gaze out over us. I could not hear his words of greeting, but the booming voice of the one he gestured to follow him was clear.

'The unanimous declaration of the thirteen united states of America. When in the course of human events, it becomes necessary for one people to dissolve the political bands which have connected them with another, and to assume among the powers of the earth, the separate and equal station to which the Laws of Nature and of Nature's God entitle them, a decent respect to the opinions of mankind requires that they should declare the causes which impel them to the separation.'

He had to pause in his reading as cheers rose and those in back pushed forward to better hear.

The man held up his hands for silence and continued, 'We hold these truths to be self-evident, that all men are created equal, that they are endowed by their Creator with certain unalienable rights, that among these are life, liberty and the pursuit of happiness.'

'It has happened – really happened!' Ben exclaimed close to my ear. Had we not been discussing this possible moment since we were too young to truly understand the full importance of it? Not knowing what to say and my throat tight with emotion, I embraced him, wondering what life would look like for us on the other side of this war for independence.

We broke apart to listen to the wrongs of King George, listed boldly by congress in their declaration.

'He has refused his assent to laws, the most wholesome and necessary for the public good. He has forbidden his governors to pass laws of immediate and pressing importance. He has refused to pass other laws for the accommodation of large districts of people, unless those people would relinquish the right of representation in the legislature, a right inestimable to them and formidable to tyrants only. He has called together legislative bodies at places unusual, uncomfortable, and distant from the depository of their public records, for the sole purpose of fatiguing them into compliance with his measures. He has dissolved representative houses repeatedly, for opposing with manly firmness his invasions on the rights of the people.'

The list went on and on. We exchanged meaningful looks when the general's man read, 'He has kept among us, in times of peace, standing armies without the consent of our legislatures.'

That was why we were here. Those troops that landed in Boston all those years ago had sparked this flame.

'For imposing taxes on us without our consent...'

I remembered reading the speech of James Otis at one of our Linonia meetings. That man could only be pleased that his argument was alive and well today.

Washington's reader had begun the document with the unbiased tone of one announcing the news, but the emotion rose in his voice as he proceeded through the many offenses of King George.

'He has abdicated government here, by declaring us out of his protection and waging war against us. He has plundered our seas, ravaged our coasts, burnt our towns, and destroyed the lives of our people.'

By the end, we could scarcely hear even his authoritative voice through the murmuring and cheering that met the final lines of the declaration.

'We, therefore, the representatives of the United States of America, in general congress, assembled, appealing to the Supreme Judge of the world for the rectitude of our intentions, do, in the name, and by authority of the good people of these Colonies, solemnly publish and declare, that these United Colonies are, and of right ought to be Free and Independent States; that they are absolved from all allegiance to the British Crown, and that all political connection between them and the State of Great Britain, is and ought to be totally dissolved.'

Our cheers were deafening and free of fear for our future.

# Chapter 36
# New York City – August 1776

*The fate of unborn millions will now depend, under God, on the courage and conduct of this army. Our cruel and unrelenting enemy leaves us only the choice of brave resistance, or the most abject submission. We have, therefore, to resolve to conquer or die.* – George Washington

Our success in stealing the British supply sloop had invigorated me, and I was eager to repeat the experience. Planning with Will and Stephen, we decided to hunt larger game. We had in mind the British warships *Phoenix* and *Rose*, which had evaded our defenses to sail up the Hudson River. Why not return to them their sloop carrying enough fire to torch one of them? And maybe Providence would guide the wind sufficiently to send both ships up in flame.

Once again, we moved under the cover of night, carefully rowing our boat full of combustibles. I had envisioned nothing besides success when a tender cruised around from behind the *Rose* and seemed pointed directly at us. Before we could react, British voices called through the still night air.

'Enemy sighted! *Phoenix* and *Rose* on high alert!'

We were not close enough to fulfil our mission, but we could take revenge upon the one who had upended our plans. We stayed on course toward the tender, sending grappling hooks over her sides before alighting the fire and making our escape in a smaller boat lashed to the side of the burning sloop.

As we rowed away, our disappointment in watching the *Phoenix* and *Rose* slowly sail away was slightly assuaged by the flames reaching into the sky from the deck of the British tender. By the time we returned to camp, wind blew and lightning flashed. We hoped that the weather would spread the flames with greater efficiency than we had accomplished but admitted that the British had likely gotten the best of us this time.

We had thought to return to our quarters with only few hours remaining before dawn, but the sky was well-lit with lightning and the wind could almost knock a man off his feet. As soon as we were out of our getaway boat, we were called in various directions as tents were blown away and a lightning strike started a fire.

The roar of thunder was as constant as the wind as swords of light crisscrossed the sky. One man who had gone to take up sentry duty insisted that I join him at his post. He was deathly pale and seemed unable to speak, so I followed him as requested.

The sight that met us made me wonder if this storm was a punishment from God for the shedding of blood that both armies were intent upon. Before me, three sentries stood, their skin black as soot and their swords melted together.

'Christ, have mercy,' I muttered as I tried to remember who had been on duty. The poor souls were unrecognizable.

I turned to the wide-eyed soldier who had fetched me and grasped his arm firmly. 'Have courage.'

He gulped.

'The lightning surely will not strike this spot twice, but we know the British are near. Keep watch, and the Lord will stand with you.' I said it automatically and hoped it was true.

He nodded and stiffened his spine. I would have laughed at his attempt to look brave, it reminded me so much of my youngest brother, but I wondered if I didn't share his frightened appearance. I nodded to him once, patted his arm, and left to arrange removal of the corpses.

It was on my way to do so that I heard of a tragedy even more horrifying than the one I had just witnessed. I felt as though I stood in the center of a hurricane as Stephen told me that another group of men, he knew not their number, had all been electrocuted when lightning struck the water filling the bunker in which they had been standing.

'God, preserve us,' I whispered, wishing that Enoch was here, for I always felt closer to the Lord with my brother at my side.

We ran about, securing tents and supplies while trying to keep a look out for the British, throughout the night. As the sun finally rose and chased the storm away, we wearily assessed the damage. The worst of it was the stories of additional men who had been struck by lightning. I had never heard of such a storm or the death of so many by lightning in a single night, but what message was hidden in this destruction? Was God angry with us or the British - or both?

As the sky brightened and thunder rolled away, one could almost believe we had imagined the violence of the storm. The vision of three poor men burnt to a crisp with their swords melted into their hands was a reminder that would remain with me for all my days.

In the days that followed, tensions rose as we waited for a British assault to fall upon us at any moment. Their ships surrounded Staten Island in such numbers that I knew most would doubt if they did not see it with their own eyes. It turned my insides watery to see the true strength of our enemy.

Washington decided that the best protection for the city on Manhattan Island was to meet the enemy at Brooklyn on Long Island. The construction of barricades and trenches there began at once, but I was disappointed to learn that my regiment was one ordered to remain and defend the city should it come to that.

'We will have chances aplenty to demonstrate our bravery, Nathan. Take heart.'

I was in no mood for Asher's encouragement and rudely ignored him. We had frozen, starved, sacrificed, and – I had thought – proven our bravery, but we were to be left behind when it really mattered. Asher's words of comfort went unheard as I stormed about my duties.

Ben found me in the midst of this tantrum and pulled me aside.

'Nathan, why do you convince yourself that the duty allotted to you is lesser than that assigned to others? Think you that we do not need to defend one of our country's greatest ports?'

I shook my head, trying to form my frustration into words.

He grasped my arms and forced me to meet his eye.

'Friend, you are better than this.' He smiled slightly to lighten this blow, and I was forced to exhale my anger and nod.

'Forgive me. You have the right of it.' I looked down, now ashamed to look him in the face. 'My brother would tell me I lack Christian humility.'

Ben's grin broadened. 'Primus was ever one to get straight to the heart of a matter.'

I laughed, but my heart ached. It would be better born with Enoch at my side, and I felt his absence ever more at Ben's mention of him.

'Perhaps I should recall that my nickname was ever Secundus and not be so reluctant to take that part.'

Ben slapped my arm. 'No need to degrade yourself, Nathan. I tell you, the duty to protect New York City is of great import, even if we do hope that the British fail to reach Manhattan's shore.'

'My thanks to you, Ben,' I muttered, my emotions still competing inside me. 'You have ever been a good friend. The best of friends, but how I do wish I was to be at your side when you march into battle.'

Ben lowered his voice and grew more serious. 'I wish it as well. I would trust my life to no other man here more than yourself, but that is not the plan God has laid out for us.' Seeing me about to retort, he held up a hand. 'Yes, it is General Washington's plan. Yet, if we do not believe that God guides his hand, why do we follow him?'

'Alright, I surrender,' I said with a sigh. 'I know better than to debate with the great Benjamin Tallmadge.'

'That's right!' he exclaimed smacking me on the back, all traces of seriousness removed from his countenance.

He strode away to oversee his men and supplies loaded onto the boats transporting troops to Brooklyn. I decided to take his words to heart and secure the city best I could, should she come under attack. As boats quietly crossed over to Long Island, I personally checked every cannon and demanded alertness from every sentry posted around the southern tip of Manhattan.

I did not see Ben again before I heard shots echoing across the water and saw smoke rising from the forests of Brooklyn.

We remained at high alert at our posts, but no British warships turned toward Manhattan. No matter how we squinted and stared, the battle taking place remained a mystery to us. Whenever a shot sounded from what seemed a different direction, we peered into the distance to discern what was happening only to eventually blame it on the sound ricocheting across the water.

Then the rain began.

We knew the muskets would become useless in the

downpour and therefore were not surprised when their racket ceased, but the silence was haunting. I imagined Ben run through with a bayonet and was not comforted by the lack of musket fire.

The rain fell in such volumes that we were forced to move tents and supplies from flooding areas and attempt to seal storehouses that held our precious powder. What miserable conditions it must have been for those at the front lines, facing the enemy with wet, useless gunpowder. I would only learn after the fact that the British had retreated to wait for the rain to end. This was when our troops began retreating across the river.

A sentry alerted me to the first flatboats rowing through the fog. By the time I arrived at shore, they had already docked, and I wondered that they had been spotted at all through the thick, dark cloud cover.

The soldiers were soaked, bloody, and muddy, murmuring about a defeat.

'Where is Washington?' I demanded of one.

'He waits for the last ship,' came the weary reply. 'He won't leave until every man has boarded a boat.'

My insides froze as I considered what this might mean. Washington could be killed or taken captive. I searched the misty waterfront for Ben. Hundreds of bedraggled men spilled from the boats, but I saw neither Ben nor the general.

The retreat continued through the night, and I was forced to take a few hours to rest to avoid dropping where I stood. Before collapsing into exhausted sleep, I prayed for Ben's safety and Washington's, too. Though his loss would not strike me so personally, I couldn't imagine a greater tragedy for our infant nation.

I awoke to a chilled morning, the grass wet with dew and a mist rising from the river. It felt refreshing after the past months of summer heat, but as I watched that mist swirling and rising, I had the feeling I was watching the souls of our lost men as they fought their way from the depths that had claimed their earthly bodies and soared away to heaven.

Boats, though not in as great of numbers, continued to trickle in from Brooklyn, with each lot arriving looking worse than the last. I questioned the sentries and others present about Washington, but they could only shrug wearily.

As the fog began to lift, a boat was revealed mid-river with a tall man standing at the prow. We instantly recognized the stance of the general, and a cheer rose from the muddy, churned up shore.

'Thank God,' I whispered to no one in particular, but I heard a few respond 'Amen.'

Men waded into the water to be the first to assist what we knew would be the final boat from Brooklyn. Others shuffled away in the realization that whoever they awaited would not be coming. I strained to make out the other faces on Washington's boat and was relieved but not completely surprised to spot Ben, grinning and standing at the very back of the boat.

Once he was within shouting distance, I called, 'I thought Washington was supposed to be the last to leave.'

Ben shrugged and held up his hands. I was thankful to see him and wished I might have known if I would have been so brave.

'You demonstrated courage and cleverness in your last two missions. In the wake of our defeat, we need to make better use of men such as yourself.'

I stood before Lieutenant Colonel Knowlton, proud to have my efforts recognized, but even more satisfied that I finally felt that my actions were making a difference. The thought that I might have given up my school, Betsey, and everything that was dear to me in return for nothing haunted me. Knowlton perhaps realized the mistake in leaving my regiment behind during the Battle of Brooklyn and offered me the opportunity to make an even greater impact on our fight against our formerly beloved parent country.

'I am forming a special force of rangers. A place in this regiment is yours if it pleases you,' he said, holding his hand out to me.

I grasped it firmly. 'It is my honor, sir. No price is too high to pay for the success of this venture and the independence of our country.'

He nodded grimly as if he was afraid the price might be higher than I anticipated, but, yes, we would render it if required.

The defeat to which Knowlton referred was worse than first realized. Brooklyn, and therefore Long Island, was lost, but we had also been forced to admit that Manhattan was indefensible under the circumstances. We planned our abandonment of one of America's largest port cities and didn't discuss how we would recover the loss.

# Chapter 37
# New York City – September 1776

*As everything in a manner depends on intelligence of the enemy's*
*motions, I do most earnestly entreat you....exert yourself to accomplish this*
*most desirable end. Leave no stone unturned.* – George Washington

I was laid low along with many others, likely the effect of
the wind and rain in combination with the poor nutrition we had
been enduring for some months. Uncertain about our position on
Manhattan after the defeat on Long Island, I felt that my illness
could not have come at a worse time. I tried to rest and do what
was necessary to regain my health as I seethed inside at the
inconvenience.

Asher, with his supernatural patience, nursed me and
brought news from around camp. Most of it was inane but helped
me to feel as though I was not left out.

'What about Knowlton?' I asked between coughing fits.
'What is the plan for his new regiment?'

For some reason, Asher appeared hesitant to share this with
me, though nothing could be more relevant than the actions of my
new commanding officer.

When pressed, Asher reluctantly admitted, 'He plots
espionage.'

I mulled this idea over in my clouded mind for a moment.
Spy work was considered dishonest and therefore dishonorable,
but if it could help us avoid losing hundreds of good, patriotic men
as we recently had, would it not be worthwhile? Clearly, Knowlton
believed so. I demanded that Asher tell me more.

He sighed and confessed that Knowlton struggled to find men willing to carry out some of the tasks he had in mind.

'Like what?'

Asher looked around the room for escape, ran his hands through his already disheveled blond locks, and then muttered, 'He wants a man to journey to Long Island to determine the redcoats' next move.'

I perked up at this. Maybe this was my opportunity. I was somewhat familiar with Long Island after my hunting trip. I could take my notes in Latin to avoid detection. Reasons this mission should be taken on piled up in my glory hungry mind, but I remained silent, not wishing to give Asher the chance to try talk me out of this course of action.

He was not fooled. 'Do you know what the man said - the one Knowlton wished to send? He was willing to go and fight them, but as for going among them and being taken and hung up like a dog, he would not do it.'

I nodded as a chill coursed through my body that had nothing to do with my illness, but I said no more.

The next day, I felt well enough to dress and go to Knowlton's quarters. Without hesitation I announced, 'I will go to Long Island for you.'

His eyebrows lifted as he looked me up and down.

'How do you know of this mission?'

'Private Wright, my waiter, informed me.'

Knowlton nodded slowly, and I realized that perhaps he hadn't wished word of a secret espionage mission to travel beyond his walls.

'Sir, I know the lay of the land and am willing to travel alone. My role as a schoolmaster is easily revived to travel without suspicion.'

He frowned as he considered my proposal. Perhaps he thought of reminding me of the danger of the mission, especially should I be captured. What would my father think of his son signing on for such a lowly position? But he did not say any of these things.

Knowlton offered his hand to me as he had not long ago, and I took it. My fate was sealed.

I strode to Will's tent, hoping he might understand why I must accept this undertaking. And because I couldn't bring myself yet to tell Ben. Part of me wished I could commune with Enoch, though I doubted he would agree with my decision. Therefore, I settled for Will. He rose as I stepped in.

'I would share with you my mission before you hear of it from others.'

Will's eyebrows rose at my blunt greeting, but he quickly controlled his face and gestured that we sit. I nodded and moved next to him.

'Colonel Knowlton has need of a volunteer.' My words failed after this brief statement. Would Will harass me as I had imagined the others would? He was simply gazing at me patiently, so I continued. 'General Washington is in need of information. I have offered to obtain it.'

Will had been about to sip his wine, and the cup paused on its way to his lips. Still, he did not speak.

'I am fully sensible of the consequences of discovery and capture in such a situation, but for a year I have been attached to the army and have not rendered any material services while receiving compensation for which I make no return.'

Slowly returning his cup to the table, Will took time to consider his response. 'You would be a spy?'

My lungs filled as I breathed deeply. 'I must. I owe my country and can think of no other mode of obtaining the information required than by assuming a disguise and passing into the enemy's camp.'

I released the remainder of the air in a rush.

Will gazed at me for a moment, looked away, and returned his focus to me before saying anything. I was beginning to wish he would fervently object as I had expected, instead of assailing me with this barrage of silence.

'I understand the patriotic ardor of your soul, my friend. However, your proposed action – the business of a spy – it involves serious consequences. Are you required to perform this duty?'

I hung my head and admitted, 'Not required, no.' Forcing myself to meet his gaze, I gave strength to my tone. 'I desire it. I am not influenced by the expectation of promotion or reward. I wish to be useful. Every kind of service necessary to the public good becomes honorable by being necessary. If my country demands this peculiar service, then I feel duty bound to perform it.'

Will did not harangue me, though I sensed his desire to do so. He considered me thoughtfully before asking, 'Who would wish success at such a price? Does your country demand the moral degradation of her sons to advance her interest?'

I felt the lopsided grin on my face. 'It is known to me that the service of a spy is not respected. It is not important. Winning our independence is all, without victory nothing else matters.'

'That such are your wishes cannot be doubted,' he quickly agreed, and I felt the muscles in my shoulders relax. 'But is this the most effectual mode of carrying them out? In the progress of the war, there will be ample opportunity to make use of your talents or to give your life to the sacred cause to which we are pledged. It is for the love of country, that I suggest this enterprise should be abandoned.'

I sighed. He had verbally outflanked me, but I would not admit it or change my course. 'Will,' I said, taking his hand. I considered confiding how dear I held his friendship, but, instead, I said, 'I will reflect upon your words and do nothing but what duty demands.'

Asher, dear boy, was not done pleading his case. 'You're too good looking to go. How will one such as you deceive? It is not your nature! Let some scrubby looking fellow go.'

I smiled and rested my hand on his shoulder. 'Your devotion is enough to warm the heart, but we are at war. I cannot pick and choose which duties are worthy of me. And who am I that I should reject anything asked of me?'

'But sir,' he would not relent. 'The powder burns on your forehead – they will recognize it as the mark of a soldier.'

'Or they will think I am a poor hunter, being that I am but a mild-mannered schoolteacher,' I countered reasonably.

Or so I thought. Asher snorted and shook his head at me as if I was a great fool. Then he took his last shot and it sent shivers down my spine.

'The boys were right all along. We thought it was jolly teasing about your birthmark, but you really are determined to hang.'

Asher ran from me then, sobbing and embarrassed, so I was not forced to respond to the only argument that had given me pause. I had the incongruent sensation of a rope around my neck while the friends of my childhood danced around me laughing about my hanging curse.

'Nathan!'

The vision dissipated and I turned to see Stephen.

'If you are determined to do this, let me accompany you.'

I had no idea how he had heard so quickly, but I was already shaking my head.

'I am to journey alone in my former role as a schoolteacher.'

He was adamant as he came closer, 'Then I shall go with you as far as possible. You should not travel this road alone.'

Knowlton and I had agreed that I would need to sail to Long Island from Connecticut, since a ship from Manhattan was easily spotted and my mission would be obvious.

'I would welcome your company until I board the ship,' I said, my heart full at the level of my friends' devotion. 'You can return with everything I am unable to carry with me.'

He nodded sternly, not pleased with my plan but content that he had inserted himself into it.

# Chapter 38
# Road to Norwalk – 14 Sept 1776

*Not for ourselves alone are we born.* – Cicero

We had not time to tarry. The British were sure to press their advantage soon, so I packed my trunk and prepared for my departure. Asher glared gloomily at me through much of these preparations, so I tried to reassure him.

'I have written to Enoch, Asher, and requested that he inform your family of your wellbeing.'

He sniffed. 'It is not I who am carelessly putting myself into certain danger.'

My laughter erupted before I could stop it. 'Friend, we are at war.'

His anger with me did not relent.

'Please, I would not have this animosity between us. Pray with me. I would have God's protection and your well wishes.'

Asher sighed and gazed at the ground for a moment. When he looked up, his face had softened. 'Very well, Nathan. In case the worst does happen, I would have the time we have together a memory that brings comfort and peace rather than regret.'

I nodded grimly, unable to deny that he was not unreasonable in considering the possibility that I might fail to return. We knelt and prayed for my safety and the success of the American cause.

When Stephen and I left for our journey, I could not meet Asher's eye and I was glad Ben had been called away on his own duties. I did not wish to begin my mission with doubts. I desired only to serve my country.

We left New York and entered the forests of Connecticut, avoiding towns and main roads. The British were not likely to intercept us on this part of my journey, but best not to tempt fate. Born and bred in Connecticut, I was content on the narrow dirt paths through heavy vegetation and felt safe as though protected by nature herself.

Some of the trees were starting to turn toward their autumn hue, but the sun was still hot above the thick, foliage canopy. I would see more color on my return trip, perhaps, depending upon how long I spent on Long Island. My hope was that I would be back with my regiment before that time.

We shot some small game along the way but subsisted mainly on hard biscuits and dried ham from our haversacks. The weather was mild enough for us to enjoy sleeping in the open under the stars.

When Norwalk's port came into view, Stephen appeared crestfallen, though this had been our objective. I knew he would board ship with me and remain at my side as long as I asked him, but, of course, I would not ask.

Before we emerged from the trees, I changed out of my captain's uniform. It felt strange to don the brown suit of my teaching days, and it fit somewhat loosely. Looking down at my shoes, I made a last minute decision to remove the silver buckles. I did not wish to draw attention to myself or lose Betsey's gift, especially now that it was likely the only one I would ever receive from her.

Stepping up to Stephen, I held out the uniform and then handed him the buckles.

'These will not comport with my character of a

schoolmaster. Please, have Asher pack them in my trunk. It is possible that you will move camp before my return. He will see that my belongings are cared for until my return.'

'He will,' Stephen murmured, taking the items from my hands. 'You are sure this is the calling God has placed upon you?' he asked quietly. He wasn't pushy but reminded me of Enoch. He might have asked if I was seeking God's glory or my own.

I wasn't sure, but I stated firmly, 'I am.'

Stephen pressed his lips together and nodded once. He had predicted my response and would not deter me further. 'Then may God go with you and safely bring you through this mission for the greater good of America.'

'Amen.'

We embraced and stepped out of the woods an onto the road to Norwalk.

It took only moments to reach the waterfront where we felt at home after our years at Yale. The sloop *Schuyler* was docked, and it seemed a prime candidate for carrying me on my way.

'What better transport than one named for one of our great generals?'

Stephen responded with a half-hearted smile.

We approached the ship and inquired of its captain.

'You will be wanting Charles Pond,' the boy we asked informed us. He pointed in the direction of a nearby tavern to indicate where we might find him.

Stephen and I thanked he boy and proceeded in that direction.

'If the name Schuyler is no great comfort to you,' I said to Stephen as we walked toward the tavern, 'you might be happier to know that I am also acquainted with Charles Pond.'

'Truthfully?' He peered at me doubtingly.

I laughed. 'Yes, I mean it. He was in the Nineteenth Connecticut before Washington rearranged the regiments.'

Stephen looked as though some of his burden lifted and he was able to walk somewhat taller. 'That is a relief to hear. Perhaps God will protect you on this mission.'

'He will be with me whether to protect me or to comfort me.'

We entered the tavern, and I spotted Charles right away. One could scarcely miss his bright red hair and bushy beard. He was of an age with Stephen and I, but his robust build and angled features made him appear older.

I approached him quietly, avoiding his notice until I was close enough to touch him. It would not do to have him shouting my name in welcome across the room. Even so, I had to gesture for silence before the boisterous greeting I saw he was about to share with me.

He exhaled loudly the breath that was meant to shout and instead almost whispered, 'Nathan, what brings you here?'

'Thank you for your discretion,' I said, gesturing toward a table in a dim corner.

We sat, and Charles tipped his head toward me and lifted a mug of ale to his mouth.

'You are captain of the *Schuyler*?'

'Aye.'

'I am looking for transport across the sound.'

He peered more closely at me. 'You are not in uniform.'

'It is necessary for my mission,' I replied.

Charles moved his gaze to Stephen, and Stephen nodded as though to confirm what Charles believed to be occurring.

'You are both welcome on my ship.'

Before Stephen could take advantage of this offer to remain

with me longer, I blurted, 'It is only I that am traveling to Long Island. Sergeant Hempstead will be returning to Manhattan.'

'Hmmm....' Charles looked thoughtfully back and forth between us. 'If that is your wish, Captain Hale.'

'Please, Nathan is sufficient for our purposes.'

Charles nodded, and I knew he certainly understood my mission now. 'As you wish,' he said in a low voice. 'The *Schuyler* is at your service.

'Thank you,' I said, hoping that he discerned the deeper feeling behind the simple words. 'I will board after nightfall, if that suits you.'

Another nod from Charles, and he returned his attention to his ale.

'Stephen, you should return.'

His eyes widened. 'Would you not have me wait here for you?'

I was already shaking my head. 'If I get as far as Brooklyn, I may find a way across the East River to return to Manhattan more quickly rather than reversing course.'

He leaned forward and lowered his voice. 'That area is swarming with British. Surely, you will return this way, especially with a trustworthy captain to provide your passage.' He tilted his head toward Charles.

It was a good point, but I needed to have the flexibility to change my plans as I went depending on what I discovered.

'I may,' I agreed. 'But in the case that I find a faster way of getting the information to Washington, you should return now.'

Stephen leaned away from me. His face was red and his shoulders tense. His jaw worked angrily as he looked from me to Charles and back again.

'I do not like this, Nathan.'

'Trust me. I will stay on a safe course. This is all for naught if I fail to get Washington the information he requires.'

Stephen released his breath and some of the color left his face.

'Fine. I will do as you wish, but, Nathan, do return this way if you can. Do not take greater risks than is sensible.'

'Of course,' I agreed easily. Once I was on my own, I would do as I thought necessary.

We drank our ale and spoke little, though I could tell Stephen had more he wished to say. He knew I was beyond changing my mind, and he therefore held his tongue. One never knew who might be listening in a crowded tavern.

When the sunset glowed red through the dust and salt coated windows, Charles stood and stretched his large frame.

'Well, boys. It's time that I readied my ship.'

We nodded, and he strode away. I turned to Stephen. 'I will go as soon as dark fully falls.'

He watched Charles' retreating form and muttered, 'I will camp outside town.' Then looking intensely at me. 'If anything – anything at all – goes wrong or makes you feel ill at ease, find me and we shall return together.'

He waited for me to agree before he would continue.

'I will begin the journey back at tomorrow noon.'

'We are agreed then.'

He did not reply, but we stood and left the tavern.

# Chapter 39
# Long Island – 16 Sept 1776

*No species of deception had any lurking place in his frank, open, meek and pious mind; his soul disdained disguise, however imperious circumstances of personal safety might demand a resort to duplicity & ambiguity. On the whole, I then thought him one of the most perfect human characters recorded in history or exemplified in any age or nation.*
– Elizabeth (Betsey) Adams Poole

I stood at the prow of the *Schuyler* as it cut through the dark water. The shadow of Long Island grew larger, as did the lump in my stomach. I tried not to consider the thought that my friends might have been right, that I was ill suited for this mission.

It wasn't too late. Even as the ship slid into the cove at Huntington, I knew I could return to Norwalk, find Stephen, and rejoin my regiment. Just the thought of doing so stiffened my resolve. How could I return and admit that I had not even tried?

I retrieved my pack and prepared to disembark.

Charles wished me Godspeed, hardly breaking stride as he moved about the ship and gave orders to his sailors. Avoiding eye contact with anyone else, I clambered over the side to the tender that would row me ashore.

The next morning, I started walking west along the north shore of Long Island. I used the road as one with nothing to hide, which felt unnatural after sneaking through the woods and cover of darkness to get here. However, now in my brown suit with my Yale diploma in my pocket, a schoolteacher would have no reason for stealth.

I attempted to recreate the laid-back ease of my steps when I had strolled into New London and leave behind my soldier's march. It felt more like playing a role than I had anticipated. How could it be such a challenge to be myself?

It was sad to realize that I was no longer that young man. I may only be twenty-one years of age, but the experience of war forces one to leave behind childish things. Yale seemed a lifetime away.

Others walking or riding along the road tipped their heads to me in greeting, but some narrowed their eyes at me distrustfully. I tried to smile openly and appear about an innocent task. Perhaps they wondered why I was not with the army, whichever side their loyalty lie.

I felt I could breathe easier when I entered a small village. Easily spotting a tavern, I went inside to acquire some dinner and listen to the conversations taking place.

My stomach groaned at the aroma of frying sausages and potatoes, and I tried to remember the last time I had enjoyed a hot meal or one that left me feeling fully satiated. Trying not to look like a starving soldier, I casually cast my gaze about the room and chose a seat that I hoped would allow me to eavesdrop without seeming obvious about it.

A buxom woman who was closer to my father's age than my own leaned over, quite clearly offering goods besides those on the menu. 'What ya hungry for?' she asked, and I hoped that a blush was not evident on my cheeks.

After I requested food and ale, she raised an eyebrow as if asking if there would be anything else, and I muttered, 'Thank you,' feeling foolish while averting my eyes and hoping it was enough to convince her to go away.

The men at a nearby table were boasting about the rebels being driven out of New York City, but I dismissed it as wishful thinking. Had I not just left that city? It had been heavily entrenched and guarded by America's best troops. However, I scrawled a reminder about Kip's Bay into my notes. These men may be blowhards, but that did not mean no truth resided within their words. Washington may wish to reinforce that landing point.

I tried to train my ear on other conversations, but it was difficult to hear anything besides these loudest voices. Instead, I focused my attention on the best meal I had eaten since my last furlough home.

The afternoon sun was hot when I left the tavern with my belly full to the point of bursting. It would do me good to get back on the road. Despite my doubts, I was nervous about the murmurs of the British on Manhattan and wished to gather more news before the day was out.

I had not gone far when a wagon caught me up and a man I took to be a farmer offered me a place on the seat next to him.

'Thank you for your kindness,' I said as I climbed up.

'I can take you as far as my farm, where you're welcome to a bed for the night. Where you headed?'

'Hempstead,' I said without thinking. The town that was also my friend's surname had come quickly to mind.

The farmer grunted a response that may have been neutral acceptance of this information, but anxiety coursed through my veins as I wondered if he thought this an odd route to take for one with a destination of Hempstead. It did not, after all, lie on Long Island's northern coast, which this road followed all the way to Brooklyn.

'At least, that is where I will go if I do not find work in Oyster Bay or Flushing,' I amended. 'I am a Latin teacher.'

'Ah.' He nodded as if this cleared things up. 'I never had much book learning myself.'

I smiled and gestured toward his load. 'It appears that you have done well with the traditional form of education.'

He smiled thinly and nodded in appreciation.

'Do you know of any schools in need of a headmaster or children in need of a tutor?'

I realized that I should have asked this of some of the residents of the previous village, but nothing was to be done for it now. The farmer was already shaking his head.

'I don't rightly know about the schools in these parts with no little ones of my own, and I don't congregate with the sort that can afford their own Latin tutor.'

'Then I appreciate your offer of a bed and will move on with the dawn.'

We rode the rest of the way in comfortable silence. I tried to avoid the temptation to doze off. The combination of the heat of the day, my lack of hunger, and the swaying motion of the wagon made it challenging, but I remained alert, watching for any sign of British troops.

When we pulled into the drive leading to a tidy farmstead, I turned to my benefactor. 'I am content to stay in the barn and not inconvenience your family.'

'No need. We have plenty of room.' He stopped the wagon and climbed down, so I did the same. When he had handed off the horses to a boy a few years younger than myself, he gestured toward the house and we walked together across a yard full of chickens.

A woman who could only be his wife, welcomed us with pleasant words and offers of cold cider, which we gladly accepted.

'Who have you brought home with you, William?' she

asked, and I realized how suspicious it was that I had not inquired regarding his name.

To cover for this mistake, I introduced myself now as if nothing was amiss. 'Nathan Hale, ma'am,' I said, tipping my head toward her. 'I am a schoolteacher.'

'How nice,' she murmured with a curious glance at her husband. 'You can get yourself cleaned up at the pump outside, and I'll have the bedroom on the left at the top of the steps ready for you by the time you're done.' She was on her way up the steep, narrow stairway before completing these instructions, so I made my way into the backyard to find the pump and remove the grime of the road from my face.

The goodwife handed me a plate of cold meat and cheese when I returned to the house, and I offered my thanks before climbing the stairs. Entering my assigned room, I was pleased with the prospect of sleeping in a comfortable warm bed. First, though, I added to my notes for the day. As a precaution, I wrote in Latin and used abbreviations for place names, making the information worthless to most men. It did not take long, for I had learned little.

I sighed as I put the sheets away and hoped for better luck on the morrow. A restful night of uninterrupted sleep was a welcome start.

Preparing to take my leave in the early morning, I thanked my host but stopped short of using his name. It was improper for me to refer to him as William as his wife had, but I knew not his surname.

'Johnson,' he said with his hand outstretched as though reading my mind. 'William Johnson.'

'Thank you, Mr Johnson,' I said, taking his hand.

'You return here if you need a place to stay . . . if you don't find a teaching position.'

I smiled and nodded, wondering if he meant more than he said and if he suspected my mission.

The road often followed the coastline closely enough that I could make note of the number of ships within Long Island's many coves. This was something at least, but I longed to discover more. Washington needed to know where ships and troops planned to go more than he needed to know the precise number anchored in Oyster Bay. Perhaps I would encounter some British troops in the next town.

I had quickly grown used to regular meals after the depravation of camp life, and my stomach growled for dinner as soon as a tavern came into view. Again, the conversation inside swirled around with stories of American defeat and retreat from New York City. When I heard multiple boasts of the British landing at Kip's Bay, I had to accept that it was likely true, and I prayed that my regiment - my friends - fought well and survived the day.

'The rebels scurry away north!' one old scoundrel laughed, and his friend joined in agreeing that, 'running away was ever Washington's strategy on the field.'

I felt my face go pale and my hunger deserted me. Was it true? Was the entirety of Manhattan Island lost? I tried to think of what information would become vital were that true. I might need to make my way into New York City if it were now held by the enemy and learn where they intended to attack next.

I picked at my food as I considered possible routes that did not include travel through Connecticut as I had come. I was determined not to return to my regiment until I had information that made my mission worthwhile. It was a good quality ale I sipped as I imagined Washington himself praising my efforts and planning his best move based upon my scribbled notes.

'Best ale on Long Island,' a man said as he took the seat next to me.

I realized I had been grinning at my daydream but agreed with him that the ale was quite good.

'These Tories make me sick,' he muttered, and I lifted my mug to avoid responding. He examined me. 'Not one of them, are you? I took you for a better sort.'

With a self-deprecating laugh, I said, 'My loyalty is to learning. I desire only a teaching position and will take my pay from whichever side is willing to provide it.'

He chortled a bit too enthusiastically, and I turned my attention to my dinner. I believed I had stayed too long and felt sweat trickle down my back.

'A schoolmaster?' he asked once he had reigned in his belly laugh.

'Aye.'

'But not from Long Island.'

It was a statement rather than a question, so I decided not to deny it.

'Connecticut, most recently at Yale.'

'A patriotic stronghold!'

He sounded proud, but I was apprehensive. I had brought my Yale diploma as evidence of my status as a schoolteacher. Would others interpret it as indication of my loyalties?

'Perhaps it now is,' I allowed, 'but I completed my studies in seventy-three.'

Before he could inquire where I had spent the previous three years, I rose from my seat and tipped my hat to him.

'I best be on my way,' I said as I left him.

Out on the street, I admonished myself to be more careful. The stranger, who I prayed was truly a patriot thinking he had found a kindred spirit, had alerted me to my need to be better prepared for questions and comments about current events. I took a deep breath and began walking at a pace fast enough to burn off my anxiety.

# Chapter 40
# Long Island – 20 September 1776

*There was no young man who gave fairer promise of an enlightened and devoted service to his country, than this my friend and companion in arms.* – William Hull

The next day when I took my seat for dinner in another hamlet along Long Island's north coast, I had prepared myself to respond to inquiries such as had been presented over the course of the previous days. I was new to this spy work, but I was determined to bring the general the information he needed.

After I had ordered an ale and sat back to observe the tavern's other customers, a man who seemed familiar to me strolled in. He appeared quite at home in the place and greeted several others before taking a seat. I searched my memory for a name or where I had seen him, for I felt certain that I had, but nothing more came to me.

Sipping my ale, I closed my eyes and listened to his voice as he made small talk with those near him. Was it familiar? I didn't think so. Maybe I had seen the man somewhere but not spoken to him. He did not seem to recognize me, so perhaps I was letting my anxiety get the best of me. I decided not to tarry in this uncertain position, forgoing the meal I had planned to order, I rose to leave.

I was surprised to be hailed by the man as I made my way toward the door. Looking at him directly, I took in the rugged features and stocky build, again trying to remember if I had seen him somewhere before. I tilted my head in greeting but did not slow my progress.

'Sit with us,' he insisted, patting the bench next to him. 'We will have enough for whist.'

Shaking my head, I smiled but apologized, 'I do not play at cards.'

'What!' he exclaimed as if he had never heard such nonsense. 'Are you one of those Puritans?'

'Congregationalist, sir.'

'And they don't play cards?' He shook his head at the absurdity.

'Well, I don't anyhow,' I explained apologetically. 'My father was adamant about it, and my brother who is training to be a preacher would be disappointed in me indeed were I to fall into such sin.' I chuckled as if I believed it was a bit silly as well.

He was still patting the bench. 'Well, sit anyway. Are you allowed to dice?'

I winced and shrugged.

'What a dreary existence,' he grumbled as he signaled to the tavernkeeper's daughter to bring a round of ale. Since he had included me in the gesture, I finally sat at his table. 'Are you a soldier?' he asked once I had.

I tried to keep my eyes from widening at his bluntness. After all, if I were a soldier, for either side, what was I doing here? I shook my head in what I believed was a self-deprecating manner and hoped that he would assume that my religion also kept me from fighting like the pacifist Quakers.

'I am a schoolteacher.'

'Ah, I should have guessed that,' he said, looking me up and down.

'Do you know anyone in need of a Latin tutor?'

He was laughing uproariously before I was halfway through the sentence. Nudging one of his friends, he bellowed, 'Do I look like I'd know anyone in need of a Latin tutor?'

They were having some fun at my expense, but I sipped my ale and took it good-naturedly. Perhaps they would talk about any British troops they had observed and this ridicule would be worthwhile.

I ordered my dinner after all and sat back to listen more than I spoke.

My new friend, who had introduced himself as Rob, a name that did not help me determine why he seemed familiar, talked about hunting, fishing, and almost every topic on earth except the British and their movements.

'I grew up near Haverhill, Massachusetts,' he said in the tone of one telling a great story. 'My parents left this world for the next on the very same day.' He looked around raising his eyebrows at us, as if daring us to doubt him. 'A hunter, sure that a bear had tracked him in the forest, shot my poor old man. Leaving the scene of that crime, he came upon my mother wrapped in her furs to stave off the hellish winter. Thinking she was a wolf, he shot her too.'

Groans and exclamations went round, and I had to concentrate on not rolling my eyes at the implausibility of his tale. I grew tired waiting for someone to say something of value and watching his dark curly hair flicker in different shades as it caught the firelight.

'Thank God those redcoats are moving their arses to Manhattan,' he grumbled as he stuffed his mouth with bread.

I had almost missed it, practically dozing after a full meal and the warmth of the room. His friends were murmuring their agreement.

'They scare off the game.'

Another man I knew only as John agreed, 'And they tear

down our fences for firewood!'

My hands itched to pull out my notes, but I tried to remain as passive as I had been throughout their conversation.

Rob laughed and smacked the table. 'With Washington's army running, the lobsterbacks will settle themselves in New York City, no doubt. Many loyalist ladies to keep them warm through the winter there.'

The men laughed and turned to other topics, but I finally had something. I laid some coin on the table to cover my portion of the fare, but before I could stand, Rob's hand clasped on my arm.

'Stay,' he commanded under his breath.

Pinpricks of panic coursed through my veins, but I remained in my seat. As if by hidden signal, it was the other men who began to leave.

'I believe our missions are one and the same,' Rob murmured to me when we were alone. He cut me off when I tried to object. 'Stop. It's unconvincing.'

I gulped and said nothing.

Leaning in close, he revealed, 'I am here gathering information for General Washington. We served together back in the last war fighting the French.'

'Is that so?' I asked, trying to buy some time to consider whether I could trust this man.

'Been scouting out the enemy's movements since the beginning,' he said smugly for someone talking about dishonorable espionage. 'Report directly to the general himself.'

That's when it hit me. I recalled seeing this man at Cambridge when we were still camped around Boston. We had not spoken nor been introduced, but that had to be why he was familiar. I almost sighed in relief.

'How did you know?' I had to ask. Thankfully, one who was trustworthy had seen through my ruse, but I had to know how I was giving myself away.

He shrugged, looking me up and down again. 'You just don't fit in.'

Now I did sigh.

'Tell you what,' he said, leaning closer, 'we are not the only patriots on Long Island. Meet me here again in the morning, and we will make a plan to work together.'

I nodded, thankful for the offer now that I realized how much I wished I had brought Asher or Stephen with me. One becomes used to being surrounded by brothers in camp. We agreed to a time and departed. I was eager for my bed and wished to feel rejuvenated for our mission in the morning.

As I prepared to climb into the threadbare bedding of the attic room I had rented, I noticed the sky had an odd glow toward the west. It was long past sunset, so I walked to the window in wonder. Upon closer examination, I was sure smoke rose in the distance. Could the patriots be burning British ships? I hoped so. That was preferred to the other thought that seared into my mind.

If Washington had been forced to abandon New York City, would he have burned it in his wake?

# Chapter 41
# Long Island – 21 September 1776

*Et tu, Brute?* – William Shakespeare

I woke early, eager to meet my fellow patriots and hopeful that they would have knowledge of what I believed was the fire burning the night before. Depending upon what information they had gathered, it might prove unnecessary for me to cross to Manhattan to discover more. I was sure it would be safer to return as I had come, but I would not shirk my duty.

It was a strange sensation to step out of doors and be greeted by the sun rising in the east and the glow of fire in the west. I was sure now that's what it was because the scent of smoke hung in the air - too much to be burning ships, which made me fear for the poor city on the southern tip of Manhattan.

I strode toward the tavern, new purpose in my step.

Rob rose from his seat to welcome me as I entered, assuring me that his friends would arrive soon. I admitted I was early because of my curiosity regarding the fire to the west.

'New York City,' he said sadly. 'Washington must have ordered it burned to avoid the British benefiting from its houses and supplies.'

I slouched back in my seat, trying to imagine the city in which I had so recently resided going up in flame, but he was clearly correct.

'It is surprising that Washington would give such an order,' I said, and he nodded but did not conjecture further.

'Have you been following the post road? Counting ships?'

he asked.

I looked around, but we remained the sole occupants of the dark room. 'Yes, from Huntington to here.'

He grinned broadly and looked up as the door opened. 'Here they are!' he bellowed, waving over three more men who were unfamiliar to me. 'I trust them with my life,' he reassured me. Once they were seated around our table, he asked if I had taken notes.

'In Latin,' I said, hoping it made me sound cleverer than my failed disguise had.

'Well done,' he said as I reached into my boot where I had stowed away my figures and observations.

'And you?' I asked as I spread them upon the table.

He leaned back when I had expected him to be keen to evaluate my notes. His face hardened. I looked to the others, but they were all watching him. He took a deep breath and leaned toward me.

'I have captured a rebel spy.'

All eyes swiveled to me, and a weight dropped into my gut.

I opened my mouth to speak. Clamped it shut. What could I say? I had laid it all before him. What a fool!

I closed my eyes, released my breath, and begged God for help.

The sound of chairs scraping across the floor informed me that I was now surrounded by my captors. I opened my eyes and met Rob's gaze.

'Not your fault, boy,' he said, almost kindly. 'I do know Washington and did offer him my services. But he declined.'

I closed my eyes again, wishing there was a way to go back – just to a few moments ago when I could have remained in my room or left town instead of meeting with this Tory gang. Then hands grabbed me and forced me to stand.

Ropes went around my wrists, and my notes were swept from the table. I heard murmurs about how naïve I had been.

They were right, of course.

My captors led me outside where more of their troop waited. They surrounded me and began marching me out of town. I listened to their banter, as if I could somehow escape and share this hard-won wisdom with the general.

I heard a familiar voice.

Craning my neck this way and that, I finally spotted the source.

'Samuel?' I whispered. I almost stumbled. I don't know if he had seen me, or if he knew only that they were transporting a prisoner. I peered through the men around me to catch another glimpse of my cousin.

Our eyes met and his hardened. If I had expected mercy or assistance, it took only that second to tell me I was still being naïve. Samuel glared at me before looking away and moving to where I could not see him.

I was forced to walk until we came to the shore of the East River. There, I was pushed into a flatboat. Smoke still rose from New York City, but I had no opportunity to mourn its loss. In moments, we were rowing toward its ashen remains.

The skyline of the city was unfamiliar as we came closer. The old Dutch houses had likely burned quickly, but stone structures remained. I wondered who had started the fire or if it had been a crazy coincidence happening when it did.

The smell of smoke was thick in my nostrils by the time we climbed out onto one of the remaining docks. I didn't see any flames, but heat still shimmered from some of the blackened debris.

I was shoved forward into the familiar but forever altered streets, and I stumbled along, trying to keep track of where we were with so many landmarks turned to ash. The sun was low in the sky, and I was shocked to realize that most of the day had been spent bringing me here, to the place I had left with visions of patriotic victory filling my mind.

My friends had been right. I had been the wrong person for the task, and I would not be the only one to suffer for it. Washington needed the information I was supposed to be gathering, and here I was. Disgraced. Humiliated.

'Major Rogers will be getting your death warrant signed,' a nameless Tory informed me. I was thrown into a greenhouse that had been stripped of everything edible that might have once grown there.

'Sir, might I have a Bible?' I asked, wondering how I could face this night.

He laughed. 'I ain't got no extra Bibles for no yankees. It's straight to hell you'll be going anyways.' Before he slammed the door behind him, he added, 'Enjoy your last night on this here earth.'

'Major Robert Rogers,' I murmured. Had I heard of him? Perhaps I had seen him in camp, but I had not considered that he might have been sent away or deserted. He had been clever and treacherous, where I had been gullible and artless. We were at war, and he had won.

I watched through the blurry greenhouse glass as the sun settled below the horizon and realized I had seen this place from the boat when we first came to New York City on that miserable rainy day. As the sky turned into a kaleidoscope of color that Enoch would have loved to see, I wondered if I would ever witness another sunset again.

# Chapter 42
# Beekman Greenhouse – 21 Sept 1776

*To study philosophy is nothing but to prepare oneself to die.* – Cicero

I took in my surroundings as they became clear in the dim light. A single lemon tree offered a sweet citrus fragrance that attempted to mask less savory scents. The greenhouse must previously have held a dozen of the delicate trees before the British had taken them, as they took everything.

As they would take my life.

A collage of memories swarmed my brain, and I struggled to sort them out. My brother. I knew how it would wound Enoch to hear of my execution, because I knew how I would feel if I were to receive such news were our roles reversed. I wished I could spare him that pain.

My eyes scanned my prison walls for an escape that I knew would not present itself. I was surrounded by an enemy army, even if I should manage to break through these walls.

What would Betsey feel when she heard that I had been hanged? Would she be heartbroken? Embarrassed that she had once enjoyed the attentions of one low enough to suffer such a fate? A secret part of her heart would mourn our lost love, I selfishly hoped. A deeper secret part might be glad that she no longer need wonder if she had made the right choice. Her husband was living and breathing next to her, and I would soon be gone.

I looked down at my body, slim and sinewy thanks to the privations of war. It was odd to think that I would soon leave it. We are taught that our flesh was no more than clothing for our soul, but at this moment I found it difficult to believe. What would it feel like to be parted from it, to become ethereal and invisible to those I loved?

My body tensed and I had to move in my limited space, to use my muscles and bones while I still had possession of them. I walked the perimeter of my prison, finding no possible breach. I lifted my knees and reached into the air, wondering at the parts as they worked together and feeling astonished that I had never before realized how amazing it was.

I remembered hopping the barrels and grinned in spite of my dire circumstances. Imagining them before me now, I crouched low, building up momentum in these glorious muscles and attempting to sear into my brain what it felt like. Would my spirit remember what it felt like to perform acts of the flesh?

My legs flexed and I leapt to the imaginary hogshead. I could hear my friends laughing and cheering, daring me to try the next one and wagering that I would fall. I squatted and jumped as high as I could, knowing it was the last time I ever would.

The transition from life to death to new life spun webs through my mind. How would it happen? What would it feel like? This basic truth that I had known all my life suddenly seemed impossible and frightening. I realized I had no idea in what form heaven would appear.

My mother would be there. That was some comfort. Would she be disappointed in the lack of grey hairs and laugh lines I had earned? Did such things matter in the heavenly realm? The infant daughter who had died with her - would I meet her as a woman grown? Would she be there at all?

A weight grew in my chest and my stomach was queasy. I ran my fingers through my hair, yanking at it, wanting to feel something, anything, while I still could. I was ashamed to admit that I was afraid, but I had no one whom to confess.

*Be still and know that He is God.*

The words from my brother, Enoch, came to me as though he had entered the dark, humid room. I cast my eyes about the space again, wondering if the Lord had granted me a miracle.

I did not see Enoch, yet I still felt comforted by his presence. I sat on the ground and closed my eyes, treasuring the feeling and not caring if it was real or conjured by my nervous mind.

'Let us recite the psalm,' Enoch whispered, so we did.

'The Lord is my shepherd; I shall not want. He maketh me to lie down in green pastures: he leadeth me beside the still waters. He restoreth my soul: he leadeth me in the paths of righteousness for his name's sake. Yea, though I walk through the valley of the shadow of death, I will fear no evil: for thou art with me; thy rod and thy staff they comfort me. Thou preparest a table before me in the presence of mine enemies: thou anointest my head with oil; my cup runneth over. Surely goodness and mercy shall follow me all the days of my life: and I will dwell in the house of the Lord for ever.'

# Chapter 43
# NYC Artillery Ground – 22 Sept 1776

*My flesh and my heart faileth, but God is the strength of my heart, and my portion forever.* – Psalm 73:26

I don't know how I had fallen asleep, but a firm kick in the side brought me quickly awake.

'Stand up, you rebel scum. Time to meet your fate.'

I coughed and groaned as I struggled to get my feet beneath me before the man was tempted to dish out additional punishment.

'Tie his wrists,' he ordered a private who quickly moved to do his bidding.

My arms were pulled roughly behind me as soon as I found my feet and was still blinking my eyes into focus.

'The prisoner is secured, Provost Marshal,' the private formally announced.

The provost marshal nodded, turned, and led the way out. I was shoved roughly from behind and almost lost my balance.

'Move, yankee,' came the growl from behind me. 'Cunningham is not one to be left waiting.'

I wondered how my fate could worsen if I tarried but stepped forward anyway to avoid meeting the ground face first with my arms bound. My eyes searched the greenhouse, as if I thought I might find Enoch or some sign that he had visited, but, of course, there was nothing. When I stepped out the door, no one would be able to tell that I had been there.

Would anyone be able to discern that I had been anywhere

else? Had I left any mark whatsoever upon the world?

The sun struck my face as I was pushed outside, and my inner ruminations fled from my mind.

'You know,' the man who I gathered was Provost Marshal Cunningham began, 'I was briefly a prisoner of the rebels.'

I did not respond, so he continued.

'You should count yourself grateful that I do not treat you as they treated me.' His steps struck the ground with greater force as his anger grew. 'Drug me behind a horse, they did, bunch of rebel scum!'

I kept my eyes to the ground and wondered at my poor fortune to be in this man's custody.

Cunningham squinted up at the sun that was already hot in the September sky and exclaimed, 'God, I hate this country!'

The private assisting him murmured his agreement, and I remained silent.

They marched me to what had been our artillery ground and now was theirs.

'You may not know this, but you've got the better of it,' Cunningham informed me. 'Those damned souls being held in the sugar house will suffer much longer than you will once that noose is tightened.'

My bowels threatened to loosen at his words, but I would be humiliated no further. I may die a spy, but I would comport myself like a Yale man.

'If I could only have a Bible, sir,' I pleaded. Cunningham only pushed me to move faster, and I blinked away tears that threatened to unman me.

We reached a position near a tree that I supposed was to be my fatal spot, because I was yanked to a sudden halt. Cunningham strode away and left me in the care of his young private. I wondered if he went to fetch my executioner or if there was any chance that I might be pardoned or exchanged. They were a coward's hopes, but I could not help it.

'Perhaps I could speak to a chaplain?' I asked my guard, but he only chuckled and spit on my shoes.

I hung my head and closed my eyes, trying to pray and hoping to recapture a bit of the peace I had felt the night before.

'Is this Washington's man?'

A man approached us, and he was the first to look at me with curiosity and pity rather than hatred and disdain. The soldier holding my rope must have nodded, because the new arrival continued.

'Might I offer him the protection of my tent?'

By the grumbling behind me, I knew he wished to decline. However, I could also see from my new friend's uniform that he was a captain, and the private dare not deny him. My rope was transferred to the officer with a reluctant mutter of agreement.

'I am Captain John Montresor,' he said as he led me to his tent. It was set up with a table and writing equipment. Maps and notes were spread about, but I did not attempt to read them. The irony that I now had at hand all the information Washington could possibly desire did not escape me.

'Captain Nathan Hale,' I introduced myself.

'I know, of course,' Montresor replied not unkindly. 'I have possession of your notes.'

He gestured toward the table and then I did look more closely. Included in the documents that must be in Montresor's writing were my own maps, ship counts, and Latin notes that had been confiscated. Among them was my Yale diploma with my name in proud, bold script.

I said nothing but looked up at him in open curiosity. Had

he not been wearing a British uniform, I could have told myself that he was a friend of my father's with his greying hair and intelligent countenance. He was thin and wiry like a tough old bird.

'You are calm,' he stated, and I felt him examine me.

'We must all be prepared to face death whenever it shall meet us, for has not the Lord warned us that we will know neither the time nor the place?'

Montresor nodded thoughtfully, never taking his eyes from my face. After a moment, he gestured again to the table.

'Might I make a few inquiries?'

I almost laughed at the absurdity of my situation. Surely, he did not expect me to offer up information.

'Do you have a wife?' he asked in a low voice.

Pressing my lips together, I thought of Betsey.

'No,' I finally choked out.

'Would you do it again?'

I furrowed my brow and looked upon his face, wondering at this odd line of questioning. 'If I had ten thousand lives, I would lay them all down.'

'And the other rebels,' he pressed, 'they share your sentiment?'

'Patriots,' I corrected him, and stood taller than I had since my capture.

Montresor nodded slowly, taking in my thrusted out chest and stiffened spine. Was he thinking I was a fool or wondering how invaders could defeat a native population with such dedication? I would never know. He returned his attention to the collection of documents.

'Is there one to whom this would be valuable?'

He held up my diploma, so much like my brother's, and my

voice refused to cooperate. Montresor watched me struggle for composure. Watched and waited.

'Might you oblige me with some writing materials?' I managed.

'You may write your letters,' he agreed, gathering up the necessary quill and ink. 'I will read them, but I will also see that they are delivered.'

'You have my gratitude,' I said, and I meant it.

Taking the paper from him, I quickly penned a note to Knowlton. I could not share anything of military usefulness, but I apologized for my failure to rejoin my regiment.

It was the letter to Enoch that caused a piercing pain in my chest. I poured out my soul to my brother, my best friend, only slightly embarrassed that Montresor would be reading it. I was beyond humiliation now. A tear dropped to the page. I brushed it away, sniffed, and offered the missives to the captain.

He took them, nodding grimly, and placed them with my diploma.

'What are you doing with that prisoner?!'

I did not have to turn to see that Cunningham had returned. The smell of rum filled the air preceding him. Montresor's face remained impassive as the angry officer strode to the tent.

'You have untied him!' Cunningham exclaimed. 'He is a rebel spy, and you are sitting down to tea?'

I could have sworn that Montresor rolled his eyes.

'I simply allowed the man to write his last letters to his loved ones.' He still held the papers in his hand.

Cunningham stole them and yelled for my hands to be tied. Looking back at Montresor, his voice became a low growl. 'You were allowing a convicted spy to write letters to his rebel cohorts?'

'Convicted, you say? I was not aware that a trial had been held,' Montresor countered, seeming not at all cowed by the red-faced man.

'No need,' Cunningham said smugly, pointing to my notes on the table. 'The man has convicted himself.' Then he turned to me. 'And he will not be given the comfort of last words to his family.'

Cunningham grinned cruelly as he tore my letters and my diploma into shreds that fluttered through the air and scattered across the artillery ground.

I felt like I had been punched in the stomach. Montresor shook his head and turned away, and I was jerked in the opposite direction, back toward the inglorious tree.

A black man was securing the noose to a strong, high limb. Perhaps he had been enslaved in the south and accepted the British offer of freedom in return for his service. He pulled on the rope with all his might, satisfied that it would hold me. That done, he positioned his ladder directly underneath, and I was shoved forward.

'God give me strength,' I whispered under my breath as my foot found the first rung.

Then another.

A bayonet at my back urged me up another.

The noose was secured.

I noticed a small crowd had gathered. A woman sobbed.

Cunningham's arrogant smile was firmly in place.

'Any last words?'

I gazed around the place that God had chosen for my last moments. Surely, I could have anticipated none of it. I gulped.

'I only regret that I have but one life to give for my country.'

My last words spoken, I saw glimpses of my life as I prepared for it to come to an end. The faces of my loved ones appeared before me, and I fixed them firmly in my memory. I would recognize them when we met again.

The smug, half-drunk voice of Provost Marshall William Cunningham interrupted my thoughts.

'Swing the rebel off!'

# Epilogue
# West Point – 24 September 1780

*I am reconciled to my death, but I detest the mode. As I suffer in defense of my country, I must consider this hour as the most glorious of my life.* – Major John André

Major Benjamin Tallmadge prodded the prisoner forward. The British Major John André had been captured during an unsuccessful scheme with American General Benedict Arnold. The plan had been for General Arnold to turn over West Point to the British, landing a major blow to the American cause. However, André had failed to return to British lines, and evidence of the plot had been discovered in the spymaster's boot.

Tallmadge had not yet been able to wrap his head around the patriot hero Arnold turning traitor. Did he think the cause was lost? Ben could take some comfort in the fact that Arnold's partner in crime had been arrested, even if Arnold had successfully escaped and turned his coat.

Ben looked at André, wanting to hate him but seeing much of himself in the man. He was also reminded of someone he tried not to think about. His anger was exacerbated by the memories that flooded his mind despite the dam he tried to force them behind. Tallmadge decided to give them release.

'I had a much-loved classmate at Yale by the name of Nathan Hale.'

He paused, his face frozen in stoic marble that refused to give the prisoner a hint of Ben's inner turmoil.

André lifted a quizzical brow and waited.

'General Washington wanted information,' Ben cleared his throat, forcing down his emotions. 'He needed to know the strength, position, and movements of the enemy.'

His eyes shot at André, leaving no doubt who that enemy was.

'Captain Hale tendered his services . . .'

Ben had to look away. He bit his lips to distract himself with physical pain and wondered how – after four years and so many other lives lost – it was still so difficult to speak of Nathan. Without looking at his prisoner, Tallmadge continued.

'He was taken.'

Forcing himself to meet André's eye, he allowed some of his anger to seep into his voice. 'Do you remember the sequel of the story?'

'I do,' André admitted quietly. He was neither apologetic nor afraid. Upon his countenance was infuriating calmness. Indifference.

Ben growled, 'He was hanged as a spy!'

He wanted to release his fury fully on the smug, condescending redcoat. Ben imagined how satisfying it would be to pummel André's face and throw him into a cellar to await General Washington's orders, but he didn't allow this fantasy to change his demeanor. He brought his features under control and stared straight ahead, even as he felt the prisoner's eyes on him. When André next spoke, Tallmadge almost smiled. There was now fear in the polished words.

'But you surely do not consider his case and mine alike?'

Ben let the question hang in the air as they marched toward their final destination. He remembered Nathan during their time at Yale and imagined his friend's body hanging unceremoniously from a tree, left there for days as a warning to those who would consider activities disloyal to their king.

When he finally looked at André, the man's face had changed. He had seemed so confident of his position. Of his charm. He no longer seemed certain of anything. He was troubled in spirit for the first time that Tallmadge had seen.

Ben cleared his throat, lifted his chin, and stated, 'Yes, precisely similar, and similar will be your fate.'

# Afterword

It is unknown when Captain Nathan Hale realized that Manhattan was lost, making his mission moot. Lieutenant Colonel Knowlton was killed in the fighting at Harlem Heights, but Hale would not have known this before he went to his own death.

Word of Hale's execution quickly reached the Americans. Captain Montresor met with an American officer, possibly Alexander Hamilton, under flag of truce to discuss prisoner exchanges and informed them that a spy named Nathan Hale had been hanged that morning. There is no record of Washington's reaction, but Benjamin Tallmadge went on to form the Culper Spy Ring on Long Island and was dedicated to successful espionage for the remainder of the war.

William Hull wrote about trying to convince Nathan not to perform his fatal mission. Asher Wright delivered Nathan's trunk to Enoch, who attempted unsuccessfully to recover his beloved brother's body. Eliza delivered a son on 18 November 1776 who was named Nathan Hale Rose. Enoch also named his first son Nathan in 1784.

It is unknown if Nathan's cousin, Samuel, was a part of his arrest, but rumors abounded at the time that he was, and he moved to England before the end of the war.

Today there are monuments to Nathan Hale, but no contemporary image of him exists.

# Additional Reading

For those interested in reading more about the historical figures featured in this novel, I recommend the following sources:

*Documentary Life of Nathan Hale* by George Dudley Seymour

*A Peculiar Service* by Corey Ford

*Nathan Hale: The Life and Death of America's First Spy* by M. William Phelps

*The Martyr and the Traitor: Nathan Hale, Moses Dunbar, and the American Revolution* by Virginia DeJohn Anderson

*Spies, Patriots, and Traitors: American Intelligence in the Revolutionary War* by Kenneth Daigler

*Reporting the Revolutionary War* by Todd Andrlik

*George Washington's Long Island Spy Ring* by Bill Bleyer

*Memoir of Colonel Benjamin Tallmadge* by Benjamin Tallmadge

*A Narrative of a Revolutionary Soldier* by Joseph Plumb Martin

# Author's Note

Intelligence officer and historian G.J.A. O'Toole pulled no punches when he said that Nathan Hale's mission 'was a thoroughly amateurish undertaking in a business that permits few mistakes.' Tragically doomed from the beginning, Nathan's story is filled with unreached potential and poignant what-ifs. Nathan might have been killed in fighting that would have left his name in obscurity with thousands of others, but he has become a national symbol of patriotism because of his sacrifice.

Facts, where they are available in Nathan's story, come from letters, diary entries, and army records. I have also utilized documentation of young men in similar circumstances during the American Revolution to fill in gaps with reasonable guesses if not historical accuracy.

Nathan really did go to Yale with his brother, Enoch, where they were good friends with Benjamin Tallmadge, and their surviving letters are a joy to read. Ben's conversation with Major John André is included in his memoirs.

The extent of Nathan's romantic attachments is unknown, but the quote from Betsey at the beginning of Chapter 39 is authentic from a testimony she wrote decades after his death. Betsey's ultimatum is a figment of my imagination.

What were Nathan Hale's last words? Did he paraphrase *Cato*? It is possible. I have included a variety of reported last words attributed to Nathan within the final chapter, since there is no way to be certain at this point if he said all or none of them.

So why did I decide to write about Nathan Hale? I was drawn to his tragic heroism and snuffed out potential, his idealism and intelligence. I wanted to write a thought provoking, emotional story that might appeal to male readers as well as female. He presented a different kind of challenge while having much in common with the women I have written about. I hope that I have honored Nathan Hale and spurred on an interest in the faith, hope, and ideals that are the foundation of this great country.

Special thanks to Cheryl Daniel of Digital Yarbs for reconstructing Nathan Hale's image based on the statue of him that stands in New York City Hall Park. Thanks to her, we are able to envision what Nathan might have looked like despite the lack of contemporary images. This special cover redesign would not be possible without her talented work and dedication to bringing history to life.

You can read more about this era in my first nonfiction book, *Women of the American Revolution*, published by Pen & Sword. Thank you for your support!

Samantha

Made in the USA
Columbia, SC
27 April 2025

57212460R00167